"My heart belo

Jacob pressed his ha... ...as Teena had done. "Mine, too."

They studied each other openly, frankly, for the first time. A sense of something he could only explain as unity wrapped about them, though he could not say if she felt the same. Only that her eyes held his, dark and bottomless, opening to him with trust. He vowed he would treat her fairly from here on. No more judging her with the same anger he judged the shaman who killed Aaron.

Life was more complicated in his world. However, he considered himself a fair man, and there was one more thing he must do to be fair.

"I would like you to help me at the clinic," he told her. The words were easier to say than he anticipated.

ALASKAN BRIDES:
Women of the Gold Rush
find that love is the greatest treasure of all.

Yukon Wedding—Allie Pleiter, April 2011
Klondike Medicine Woman—Linda Ford, May 2011
Gold Rush Baby—Dorothy Clark, June 2011

Books by Linda Ford

Love Inspired Historical

The Road to Love
The Journey Home
The Path to Her Heart
Dakota Child
The Cowboy's Baby
Dakota Cowboy
Christmas Under Western Skies
  "A Cowboy's Christmas"
Dakota Father
Prairie Cowboy
Klondike Medicine Woman

LINDA FORD

shares her life with her rancher husband, a grown son, a live-in client she provides care for and a yappy parrot. She and her husband raised a family of fourteen children, ten adopted, providing her with plenty of opportunity to experience God's love and faithfulness. They've had their share of adventures, as well. Taking twelve kids in a motor home on a three-thousand-mile road trip would be high on the list. They live in Alberta, Canada, close enough to the Rockies to admire them every day. She enjoys writing stories that reveal God's wondrous love through the lives of her characters.

Linda enjoys hearing from readers. Contact her at linda@lindaford.org or check out her website at www.lindaford.org, where you can also catch her blog, which often carries glimpses of both her writing activities and family life.

LINDA FORD

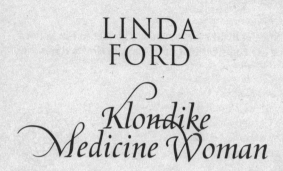

Klondike Medicine Woman

Love Inspired

Special thanks and acknowledgment to Linda Ford
for her contribution to the Alaskan Brides miniseries.

Recycling programs
for this product may
not exist in your area.

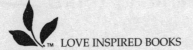 LOVE INSPIRED BOOKS

ISBN-13: 978-0-373-82867-8

KLONDIKE MEDICINE WOMAN

Copyright © 2011 by Harlequin Books S.A.

www.LoveInspiredBooks.com

Printed in U.S.A.

But God commendeth his love toward us, in that, while we were yet sinners, Christ died for us.
—*Romans* 5:8

To Tom, Yvonne, Jordyn and Chris
for sharing our trip to Alaska and Yukon.
You made it a memorable event. Thank you.

Chapter One

July 1898, Treasure Creek, Alaska

These people were set on destroying not only the land but themselves, as well.

Teena Crow bent over the injured man. Blood pooled under his leg, a fresh stream joining the black patch in the grass. If she didn't stop the bleeding soon, he would die beside the Chilkoot Trail like so many others had. She took in his pain-filled eyes, the way the color seeped from his cheeks. Shrugging out of her fur shawl, she wrapped it around him then took out the reindeer moss, the plant known as mare's tail and other healing remedies she always carried with her. She carefully packed the wound. The blood flow stopped immediately. She watched it a moment then returned her gaze to the man, wondering if he would say with his eyes or mouth, or both, what he thought of a native tending him.

Many she'd helped showed no appreciation nor spared their hatred of the people who were here first.

The man's eyes were already losing their fear-filled pain and he showed nothing but gratitude.

She smiled. "How long have you been here?"

"Since first light," he croaked.

Light came early in July. That meant he had been there up to twelve hours. Teena held her canteen of water to his lips and he drank heartily. She sat back on her haunches and looked about.

All winter, they had come in boats of every sort in a mad race for the gold fields. They had flung themselves into the water, headed for land like fish thrown up at the knees of the newly formed town of Treasure Creek, Alaska, founded by Mack Tanner. They brought with them a mountain of goods that soon lay scattered across the beach. They clawed their way up the Chilkoot toward the lake and onward. They paid Tlingit Indians like her brother to pack their belongings over the pass where the Canadian Mounties waited to make sure they had the required amount of supplies. All for the glittering gold.

She shook her head. She would never understand the white man. But she had vowed to learn their ways of curing their diseases.

This was not the first one of their kind to be ignored at the side of the trail, as hundreds passed by without once pausing to help. Last winter her brother, Jimmy, had tossed his pack aside and left the path to pick up a man with a broken leg who had lain there all day without anyone helping. Jimmy brought him down the mountain to Teena. He had lived, though he might never walk as well as he once had.

There were many who got help too late.

She checked the man's wound. No longer bleeding.

He sucked in air in a way that said his pain had let up.

"You will need to rest a few days—" she began.

"Step aside," a firm voice ordered, interrupting her suggestion that the man should rest until his wound healed.

Teena didn't move except to turn to stare at the man who spoke. A white man, of course. She'd known that immediately. Over time, she had gotten used to the strange appearance of these people. But this one was different. Eyes brown as spring soil, a little furrow they called a dimple in his chin. A strong face. No head covering, so she got a good look at his close-cropped, dark hair.

As she studied him from under her lowered lashes, something inside her uncurled like a flower opening to the brilliant sun.

He edged her aside and spoke gently to the man. "I'm Dr. Jacob Calloway—a medical doctor. You're in good hands now."

Teena dismissed the way he said the words—as if the injured man was in danger of dying before he arrived. All she cared was he said he was a doctor. A white healer. She'd heard such a man had gotten off a boat a few days ago. This was what she needed. What she'd prayed for, not knowing if God would listen to her prayers. Yes, the missionary, Mr. McIntyre, had assured her the Great Creator heard the Indian as much as He heard the white, but she wondered how he could be so certain. Had he ever been a Tlingit and asked for something? How then could he know?

She would watch everything this newly arrived man did, and learn his way of healing.

A boy almost as tall as the doctor stood at his side. He had the eagerness of a child, the height of a man, but not yet the weight. No longer child. Not yet man. With an eager, yet cautious expression. He seemed to belong to the doctor. Perhaps his son, though there was no resemblance. The boy-man was as fair as the doctor was dark.

Dr. Calloway pulled something from his pocket and put a plug in each ear as he pushed aside the injured man's shirt to press a tiny, cup-like thing to his chest. He then leaned forward and listened.

What did he hear? Was this their way of healing, or was there more?

The doctor straightened, folded his instrument and placed it back in his pocket. "Now let's have a look at this gash." He made to pull the moss off.

Teena captured his hands, gently stopping him. "You must not lift it yet. It needs time to work."

Dr. Calloway gave her a faintly reproving look. "No doubt you mean well, but this requires proper medical care."

She knew nothing about the white man's methods.

But she knew how to treat a cut. "If you take it off it will get…" She struggled for the English word but couldn't find one, and had to settle for describing what would happen. "It will get red and oozy."

"Exactly." He turned his attention back to the injured man. "You need to keep your wound clean. I have some dressings with me." He again began to pull off Teena's work.

The man sat up. "I'm feeling a whole lot better. Whatever this girl did has worked. I'm heading back up the trail." He pushed to his feet.

Jacob stood, too. "You'll end up losing your leg if you aren't careful."

"I guess I'll take that chance." He limped away, Dr. Calloway at his heels, as if he meant to stop him.

The gold seeker paused as he remembered Teena's fur around his shoulder. He pulled it off and handed it to the doctor. "Give this to the little lady, and my thanks."

Jacob stared after the man.

Teena shared his sense of helplessness, but had long ago learned people did not always listen to advice, no matter how wise.

"I fear you will get infection," he called to the man's back as he limped up the trail. "If you do, please come back to Treasure Creek. I am going to start a medical clinic."

A medical clinic. White man medicine. Teena's heart soared. She would offer to help. She'd do anything he asked, if he would only teach her his ways.

The doctor returned to Teena's side. He slipped her shawl over her shoulders, caught her two braids and lifted them from under the fur. He performed the task naturally, his thoughts obviously elsewhere, but his touch gave the pelt gentle warmth, as if from the noon-day sun. For a moment she closed her eyes and enjoyed the comfort.

"I'm going to ask you to stop using your primitive practices on these people."

Teena slowly turned to stare. "What do you mean?"

"Ignorance kills many." His expression tightened, marring his strong face and filling his eyes with hardness, but Teena did not back away. She needed this man's help. Besides, she agreed. Thousands had come seeking the glittering gold—unprepared for the cold, the mountains or any of the dangers. Far too many perished, and hundreds more sat defeated and broken at the edge of the water.

"These people deserve proper medical care." He picked up his black leather bag and turned back toward Treasure Creek, the boy-man matching his gait stride for stride. He grinned at his young friend. "Seems I got here just in time."

The boy gave Dr. Calloway an admiring glance.

"You are going to do white man's medicine?" she asked.

Jacob did not slow his steps, forcing her to hurry to stay at his side. He was a tall man. Taller than most she'd seen. And he walked with purpose. The boy hurried to keep up, too. "That's why I'm here."

"You will need help at this clinic?" She congratulated herself on remembering the word.

"I trust there are those who would be interested in assisting me." He smiled again at the boy.

She rushed onward. "I am Teena Crow of the Tlingit tribe. I will help you."

He stopped. For a moment he didn't move, then he faced her, his expression like granite. "Do you know scientific methods?"

Not certain what he meant, she shook her head.

"Are you willing to abandon the practices you've been taught?"

She did not answer directly. "I want to learn more."

"I'm afraid I can't help you." He strode on.

His words—although softly spoken—were like blows to her. This was what she had longed for, hoped for and prayed for. He was several yards ahead of her and she ran to catch up. "I do not understand."

"Your people's ignorant ways have killed many. Now that I'm here, I can save others from such malarkey." He continued to the busy town that hadn't existed a few months ago.

Teena stared after him. She must have misunderstood him. Or he had misunderstood her. She followed the pair slowly, at a distance, as they made their way to the center of town. Jacob paused at the church—the first building Mack Tanner had constructed. Now he was adding to it to allow more people to attend services. Across the street stood another building—the school. They taught children to read and write. Mack said the native children were welcome to learn along with the whites, but the Indian children had accompanied their families to the fishing streams and helped with drying fish for the winter.

Teena wished, not for the first time, she could read. Then she could learn how to treat white man's diseases without need of a teacher.

Dr. Calloway hurried onward to the street opening to the waterfront, the boy still at his side, pointing and talking. The store on the left did not draw the doctor's interest. Instead, he turned to the empty space across the street. Was this where he intended to have his clinic?

The man-boy spoke, waving his arms wildly. The doctor nodded and the boy hurried toward the waterfront and the throng of people and supplies.

Teena would never get used to the scurrying crowds, the unending noise, the strange smell of so many unfamiliar things.

She hung back, watching as the doctor paced the piece of land.

"What are you staring at?"

She didn't take her attention from the scene before her as she spoke to her brother, Jimmy. "Him." She pointed. "Dr. Jacob Calloway. He's going to start a white man's place for healing." They had automatically fallen into their native language.

"More white men. Just what our land needs."

"We must accept the changes. Learn how to work with them."

"Who says?"

"We see what happens if we stick to our old ways."

"If they hadn't come, our people wouldn't have died of strange diseases."

"But they did come. Our people did get sick." She shuddered at the memory of one after another of her clan dying, their skin marred by the dreaded pox. "We need their medicine to cure their diseases."

Jimmy didn't answer. They disagreed on so many things, but he had no argument for this. "I wish they had never come."

"We cannot push the sun back one hour, let alone the days and weeks it would require to go back to who we were before the white man came."

"They have brought us a curse."

She studied him, her face happy with a smile. "They brought us the news that we can know the Creator. We have always known about Him but feared His anger. We did not know He had sent His Son to open up the way for us to lift our hearts to Him."

Jimmy's face darkened. "Sometimes I think He is angry at us for being so bold. That is why we are punished with diseases we can't conquer, and the swarm of people seeking gold, who care not about the land."

Side by side they stared at the mud and confusion around them.

Teena had her share of doubts, too, but she wasn't about to confess them to Jimmy. So many times, she wondered if God loved her people as much as He did the whites. "I asked for a chance to learn their healing way. I believe Dr. Calloway is what I need."

"He will teach you?"

She sighed inwardly, not wanting Jimmy to know what Jacob had said. "God has sent him. He will teach me."

"Let us hope you can learn what our people need."

"Let us so pray."

"I have to get back to work. There's no end of people willing to pay for someone to take their goods up the mountain." Jimmy's voice grew strong with pride. Day after day, he packed a hundred-pound burden up the trail in return for gold.

"I notice you don't mind taking the white man's gold."

"It is in our land. It is our gold."

"Can you eat it? Can you wear it to keep you warm? Can it cure a dying child?"

Jimmy took a few steps away, then turned to face her. "Trading with the white man takes gold. Did you not say we have to change?" He strode toward the waterfront, found the man he sought amidst the confusion and shouldered a heavy pack.

Yes, they had to change. Learn new ways.

She turned her attention back to Jacob. He stood on the boardwalk and stared around him.

She saw his careful assessment. Then his gaze rested on her. Again she felt a quickening of her heart. As if the future held a thousand unspoken promises. As if she had set foot on a bridge over a deep valley—a bridge between two worlds. As if God had heard and answered her prayer, just like Mr. McIntyre had said He would.

Jacob continued to study her.

Her skin grew warm and prickly. Perhaps now was not the best time to try to explain why she must learn his ways. Let him get used to the idea first. She turned and retraced her steps to the edge of town. She passed the dwelling place of Viola Goddard and paused to consider how anyone could abandon an infant. It was unthinkable. Her people protected their young, knowing the future lay with them. Yet someone had simply left a baby on Miss Goddard's doorstep, with some gold nuggets to provide for her care. As if gold could make up for family, a clan. How strange these people were. Yet learning some of their ways was essential for her people to survive.

She resumed her journey, following the trail through the trees to her village.

Jimmy came home later in the day. "I thought you would be with the doctor. They brought a man down from the mountain who almost cut his foot off with an axe."

Teena sprang to her feet. This was her opportunity to help, to watch and learn. "I will go now."

Her father coughed. Did the white man have a cure for this troubling affliction of her father's? He'd once been so strong and proud. He was still proud and strong in his mind, but his skin hung on his body and he moved like an old man. "Teena, daughter, do not think you can become white."

She stopped and slowly turned. "Father, I only want to learn what we need to survive."

"Perhaps you are right." He waved her away, coughing with the effort.

She scurried from the winter house. Normally, they would have all moved to the fishing camps, but this year only a handful had gone. Only a handful were well enough. Jimmy stayed to work for the gold hunters. Father had survived the pox, but it had left him too weak to hunt or fish. Teena remained behind to care for him and learn the white ways, so she would know how to help him get better. She trotted noiselessly to Treasure Creek. A crowd gathered on the walk before the place where she had last seen Dr. Calloway, and she guessed they had a reason to be hanging about.

She pushed through them to observe.

A miner held a mask over the man's nose and dripped some sort of liquid to it. Not only was his foot torn, his stomach was ripped deeply.

She groaned inwardly. A man did not survive that kind of injury.

But Jacob sewed the layers back together. The man didn't move, though she couldn't imagine the depth of his pain.

Teena edged closer, but, at a warning glance from the doctor, went no farther. She could see from where she stood. What had Jacob used to render the man so motionless? If not for the way his chest rose and fell, Teena might have thought him dead. The white doctor had a powerful medicine for pain.

Her eyes followed his every movement. He was so intent on what he did. So sure. His fingers steady. Healing hands. She could barely take her gaze from them, but spared a quick glance at his face. His expression led her to think he was both concerned about the man and determined to fix him. Teena understood the feeling of wanting to overcome injury and illness. She also knew the frustration of failing.

Jacob finished and put on a spotless white piece of cloth, then turned his attention to stitching the man's foot. An axe, they had said, but the foot was torn badly and looked more like the man had caught his foot in something powerful. Besides, how would he accidentally cut his stomach with an ax? It made her wonder if he'd been in a fight with another man brandishing a weapon of some sort. She'd often enough noted how the white man could turn on his friends and try to destroy them. This man looked as if someone had tried to tear him apart.

Dr. Calloway finished and straightened. "He'll live and likely walk again."

The crowd cheered.

At the doctor's signal, the man stopped letting the liquid drop to the mask.

"Did I hear there was a doctor here?" A voice called from the back, and a burly man pushed forward. "You a doctor?"

"I am."

"My wife is in poor shape. Come and help her."

Dr. Jacob glanced around the crowd. "I need someone

to stay with him until he comes out of the anesthesia. Who will help?"

Anesthesia. Teena had never heard of it. Was that what he did to make the man sleep through being sewn together?

The crowd melted away amidst murmurs of having work to do. Soon there was only the impatient man who sought Jacob's help, Teena, Jacob and Wiley, a wizened old man who had spent too much time lost on the mountain and now rambled nonsense. Someone had brought him down the trail a little while ago. Mack's kindness kept him alive.

"I can help," Teena murmured.

Jacob acted as if he hadn't heard. "You, mister, can you watch this man?"

"His name is Wiley," Teena offered. "He left his mind on the mountain."

Jacob gave her a quick glance, then shifted his attention back to Wiley. "Wiley, can you help?"

Wiley looked far away, as if seeing his many days lost and alone. "It's cold. The wind fair tears at a man's soul." Wiley shuddered. He brought his gaze back to Dr. Jacob. "It stole mine. It did." He turned and shuffled away, mumbling about finding his lost soul.

"Doc, hurry. My wife needs you now."

"I will stay with him." Teena stepped forward. "Or I could go with—" She indicated the pacing man.

Jacob looked as if he would about as soon cut off his own foot. He glanced at the sleeping man. "I don't seem to have much choice. He will likely vomit when he comes to. Make sure he doesn't choke." He bent to plant his face a few inches from Teena's. "You are not to give him any of your stuff." He indicated the bag slung over her back. "Do you understand me?" His words were quiet, meant only for her ears.

"I am not deaf," she muttered.

"None of your superstitious rituals, you hear?"

Teena turned her back and squatted by the injured man. She would not agree to anything she didn't want to, and this was one of those things. He might know about his kind of medicine, but she knew about her kind.

"I would not let him suffer if I could help."

Jacob squatted at her side. "Listen to me. I expect you are only following the practices that have been handed down through generations, but they are outdated. There are better, safer ways of treating the sick and injured."

"Then teach me them."

"You must first be willing to abandon your old ways."

She considered the options and shook her head. "How can I, when I know they work?"

"Doc? Come on."

Jacob made a rough sound of exasperation and followed the man.

Jacob Calloway returned to the rough wooden sidewalk and stomped the mud from his boots. This place was a disaster. In the few days he'd been here, he'd seen nothing but mud and ignorance. The woman he'd visited needed a better diet to relieve some of the symptoms responsible for her pain. He guessed her biggest problem was she really wanted to go home.

His boots thudded on the plank sidewalk fronting the row of businesses, though from all appearances, one would conclude most of the transactions were conducted on the rowdy beach. Which is where Burns Morgan had disappeared. The boy had attached himself to Jacob on the ship, and seemed in no hurry to join the climb over the mountain toward Dawson City and the gold fields. Only sixteen years old, he doubtless liked the idea of adventure more than the reality of it. Jacob didn't mind in the least, providing a bit of guidance and protection to the boy.

Jacob could have used him to watch the patient he'd sewn together a short time ago. Instead, he'd been forced to accept the only volunteer. That Indian woman.

She was not what he expected at all. A dusky-skinned beauty with big, dark eyes that seemed to delve into the deep recesses of one's mind. Her flawless skin reminded him of silk and satin. No—something warmer. Alive. He shook his head to stop his foolish thoughts, but they immediately returned to recounting each detail of that moment on the trail.

She had twin braids which seemed to be traditional. Every native woman he'd seen wore her hair in exactly the same fashion. Only, on her it looked vibrant. He'd been surprised by the warmth and weight of them.

His steps slowed. Why was he giving her so much thought?

He intended to discourage further contact. If only someone had intervened when his brother was injured... forbidden the native to treat him... It was too late to save Aaron, but he intended to do his best to save others from the same fate—death by ignorance and superstitious ritual.

Despite his insistence Teena only watch the patient, he had no assurance she wouldn't do some little dance, wave a rattle over him and sprinkle him with ashes and blood as soon as Jacob turned his back. He picked up his pace. His patient would be in need of pain medication by now. And nauseated from the ether.

He had come to fulfill a promise to his dying mother. Not that she would know if he kept his word or not. But he would know, and his conscience would give him no peace until he got on a boat from Seattle to Alaska. He intended to set up a medical clinic, train a nurse or two to care for patients and advertise for a doctor to take his place. Many doctors had left their practices to chase after Klondike gold. Surely, one would be wanting to return to medicine. When he accomplished all this, he would return to his practice in Seattle.

Jacob was close enough now to see the patient and the woman. She was taking something from her pack. Or was she putting something back? He broke into a run. "Stop. Get away."

She turned, a smile beaming from her.

He almost stumbled. A giant invisible fist slammed into his solar plexus. What would it be like to have such a smile greet him every day? He scrubbed the back of his hand across his forehead, forced his senses into order and closed the remaining twenty feet between them. He glowered down at her, but couldn't remember what he meant to say.

Good grief. He was thirty-two years old and acting like Burns, simply because a woman—a very young woman—had smiled at him. Why, she couldn't be much older than Burns.

His insides churned at his stupidity.

"I told you not to give him any of your superstitious concoctions." His frustration made him speak more harshly then he meant to. He dropped to his knees, flipped open his bag and reached for the laudanum to provide the man pain relief. Then he realized his patient rested quietly. No complaint of pain. No retching. "What did you give him?" He checked the man's pulse and reactions, but apart from being comfortable, he detected nothing amiss.

His patient opened his eyes and focused on Jacob. "Hi, you must be the doctor. Teena here told me how you sewed me up without me feeling a thing."

Teena. For some reason, the name suited her. She seemed keenly interested in medicine. If only she would agree to abandon her old-fashioned ways, based on superstition and tradition rather than science, he might consider training her as a nurse. But she'd been very clear she didn't intend to. He did his best to ignore her, and instead spoke to his patient. "What's your name?"

"Donald Freed. Thanks for fixing me up, Doc."

"Did this woman give you something?"

Donald's smile was mellow to say the least. "Whatever it was, it took away the pain."

Anger roared through Jacob like a raging storm, destroying everything in its path. His brother had died not far from here, with a native caring for him. If Aaron had received proper medical care he would likely still be alive. Instead he'd been deprived of modern medicine, and worse, poisoned. He jolted to his feet and grabbed the young woman by the arm. "What did you give him?"

Her eyes widened but she showed no fear. Perhaps it was compassion filling her expression with such warmth.

Ashamed of his behavior, he dropped her arm and stepped back. "Tell me what it is so I can know how to counteract it." He feared the ignorant cures of these people would poison Donald as it had Aaron. "Tell me before it makes him sick."

Teena smiled, gentle and reproving. "It is only all-heal root. It will not make him sick. It will make him comfortable. Happy."

"Doc, I feel great. Happy, like she says."

Who knew what Teena had fed the man? Or the consequence. Frustration twisted with Jacob's anger. How was he to combat ignorance if men like this encouraged it? His only hope was to insist Teena stay away from the clinic. He leaned closer to Teena, making sure she heard and understood every word. "I want you to stay away from the sick people. I will treat them."

She didn't move an inch. Her eyes didn't so much as

flicker. "You need my help. I need yours. I have prayed for a chance to learn the white man's ways of healing. You will help me and I will help you."

"Not in this lifetime," he vowed.

She smiled and calmly walked away. "We will see each other again."

He groaned. Was this some kind of punishment for an unknown omission of his? Was God testing him to see if he would falter?

I will not fail in keeping my word to Mother. I will do my best to bring proper care to these people who are seeking their fortune in gold. Then I will return to my pleasant life in Seattle.

His resolve strengthened, he again checked Donald, who rested comfortably. Then he pulled out paper and pencil and started a list of what he needed.

A little while later he entered the general store and spoke to Mack Tanner. "I'll need these supplies to build the clinic. And I need to hire someone to construct it for me."

Mack was the founder and mayor of the town. He had strict regulations against saloons and dance halls. He'd built a church in the center of town to signify that, in this place, God was honored. Knowing Treasure Creek was established on moral principles had been the reason Jacob had chosen this particular location to set up a new practice. Plus, the letter informing them of Aaron's death had stated that Aaron was buried here.

Mack took the list and nodded. "I have the building material at hand. I'll have it delivered to the site."

"I'd appreciate that."

"As to someone to do the work…" He shook his head. "Most people are trying to get to the gold fields. Now, if you've no objection to a woman doing it…?" He let the unspoken question dangle in the air.

Jacob could think of no reason to care who did the construction and said so.

"Then I'll ask the Tucker sisters to help you. They're kind of jacks-of-all-trades."

"Fine. The sooner the better. It's hard to provide adequate care out in the open."

"For sure. How about a tent for now? In case it rains." He glanced out the window. "Which it's bound to do soon."

"That would help." A short time later, he left with the promise of delivery of tent, lumber and other supplies, though much of what he needed in the way of supplies had to be ordered, with no assurance of when they'd arrive.

He hurried back to the place where his clinic would soon stand. Two men brought over the tent and erected it and helped him move Donald under its shelter, then delivered the lumber, and the news that the misses Tucker would show up in the morning. Despite the urgency he felt, he understood this was the most he could hope for. Soon he would offer adequate medical assistance. No longer would the injured and ill have to depend on superstitious claptrap.

He smiled as he recalled Teena's quiet stubbornness. She would soon learn she was no match for his determination. And why that should make him chuckle he was at a loss to understand.

He looked into his cup of coffee. Had she secretly poured in some kind of native drug that would make him anticipate a duel of wills with a native?

Snorting at his foolishness, he tossed the rest of the coffee into the dirt.

Chapter Two

At the sound of voices close to his head, Jacob was instantly awake and paused to orientate himself. He'd slept on the ground, softened by furs Mack had sent him. Burns had returned about 11:00 p.m., all wound up because it stayed light so late.

"A person never needs to go to bed."

"You'll want to sleep sometime." Jacob wasn't sure he'd ever been so enthused about staying up all night. Or so eager to experience life.

He glanced across to where Burns had thrown himself down on his own soft fur and lay snoring gently, his arms outflung like a baby. He didn't look as if he meant to leave his bed in search of adventure for several more hours.

Jacob smiled, a feeling of affection and protectiveness warming his insides. He'd grown fond of the boy. Perhaps Burns reminded him in a small way of Aaron—young, naive, so certain adventure carried no risks.

Maybe Jacob could make up for not being able to protect Aaron by keeping Burns out of danger.

The noise outside his tent grew louder and Jacob scrambled from his covers. He checked Donald. Several times in the night, he'd risen to tend the man, who rested quietly at the moment. A quick glance at his pocket watch, where he'd left it on a small table by his makeshift bed, revealed it was—

He grabbed his watch and held it to his ear. Yes, it ticked. He wound it to make sure. Four in the morning, and yet the racket outside gave him reason to think it was high noon. One voice called, "Right there is good, boys." It sounded as if the speaker was only a few feet away. A crash fairly rocked him where he stood. Burns grunted and rolled to his side. Donald started, moaned and sank back into oblivion.

Jacob took a moment to smooth his hair. His chin was rough with whiskers. At some point he needed to shave. But first he had to find out the cause of the commotion outside. He pushed aside the tent flap and slapped at the cloud of mosquitoes attacking him.

A handful of men, nudging each other and jeering, stood watching two people struggle with armloads of lumber.

"Frankie, hang on. It ain't that heavy," one of the wood-toting persons called.

"You wait until I get a good hold, and don't drop it without telling me. You left me holding the whole thing," Frankie sputtered as he rubbed his palm.

"Daylight is wasting." The second person tapped a

mud-covered boot and glanced at the sky, as if to suggest the sun was crossing the sky at a furious pace.

"You tell 'er, Margie," one sunburned man yelled.

This was a woman? And Frankie, too? The women Mack had said would help? Jacob took a good look at the pair. Both had dark, short hair—or at least what he could see of it, hidden by knitted caps, suggested so. Both dressed in plaid jackets that seemed to be uniform for both native Alaskans and the bulk of the outsiders. And both stood with feet planted a good width apart.

"You gonna take that from your sister, Frankie?" another spectator called. "Come on, show her who's boss."

Plainly, the onlookers hoped to see a fight between the two. In fact, he figured the men itched to get a good brawl going. Jacob took a step forward, hoping to prevent such a thing.

The one called Frankie closed the distance separating her from her sister, her expression dark and forbidding.

The men cheered.

Frankie stood in front of her sister and planted her hands on her hips.

The cheering intensified.

Jacob held his breath, wondering if he'd be handing out dressings in the place of his future clinic.

Both women let out a whoop that sent shudders down Jacob's spine and, laughing uproariously, threw their arms around each other, administering vigorous back pats.

The crowd muttered their disappointment and most of them moved off to attend to their own affairs. That's when he saw the Indian woman again. Teena Crow, she had said was her name. Her dark eyes watched him with unwavering purpose. *I will help you. You will help me.* His face felt brittle. His eyes stung as he silently signaled his determination. It would not happen. He had come to provide scientific medical care. He tipped his chin in a gesture that said he wanted her to leave. She held his gaze without a flicker of concern.

Frankie and Margie watched the silent exchange. Then one stepped forward. "Margie Tucker at your service. Mack said you wanted someone to put up a building. This here is my sister, Frankie. She might lend a hand if she can manage to hold up her end."

He shook hands with the pair. "Appreciate your help." He glanced toward the last place he'd seen Teena. Only to check that she'd left, he assured himself. She was indeed gone. He glimpsed her heading down the trail leading over the mountain, her graceful gait unmistakable even at this distance. He felt satisfied she had moved on, though somewhat disquieted—only because he'd been rude. Out of necessity, he firmly explained to himself. He turned back to Margie. "I've got a young man with me who will assist you." He would pay Burns to work. Perhaps it would provide incentive for him to stay in Treasure Creek, rather than heading to the gold fields.

"The more the merrier. 'Specially as our younger sister seems more interested in her new husband than in giving us a hand." Margie's words growled out, making it sound as if having a husband was worse than having the plague. She turned to Frankie. "Why'd you let her up and marry Caleb anyways?"

Frankie sputtered. "I tried to convince her no Tucker woman needs a man, but you saw how stubborn she was."

Margie and Frankie rolled their heads and scratched their hairlines in mutual sadness.

Then Margie laughed. "We'll be glad of your friend's help. It'll make the job go faster, too. Now show us what you have in mind, so we can get to work while the sun shines." She roared with amusement.

Seeing his surprised and somewhat stunned reaction, she patted his shoulder. "My idea of a little joke. In the summer we have no shortage of sun." She slapped at the mosquitoes. "Nor these little blighters. You get yourself some of that stuff Teena Crow makes up. It helps keep them off."

"I don't want her around here."

The pair gave each other a glance rife with secrets. "You got something against her?" Margie's voice was soft, but Jacob didn't miss the warning note.

Not knowing the situation well enough to venture too far, he heeded the warning. "I'm a medical doctor prepared to use my understanding of scientific principles to help people. That woman's methods are based on superstition and—"

Margie nudged Frankie hard enough to cause her to stumble. "I think our city doctor will soon learn the difference between what matters and what doesn't. Don't you think so?"

Frankie guffawed. "There's those that look only at the outside and judge. Don't we know that?"

The pair slapped each other on the shoulders and laughed.

Margie grabbed some stakes. "Now, where do you want the building?"

He showed them what he had in mind and helped them stake the corners. When they finished, he went into the tent and nudged Burns from his sleep. Last night, when Jacob offered to pay him, the boy had eagerly agreed to assist with the construction.

"What's wrong?" Burns mumbled, burrowing deeper into the comfort of his bed.

"I thought you wanted to help." It was imperative to get the building up as soon as possible.

Burns groaned but made no move to rise.

"I can think of ways to make you get up." Jacob stood over the boy, remembering the times he'd teased Aaron to get him out of bed. "I used to toss cold water in my brother's face when he refused to wake."

Burns squinted through one eye. "You wouldn't."

Jacob shrugged. "Not if you get up on your own."

Burns moaned. "Is it even morning yet?"

"Open your eyes. Daylight is burning."

A crash of dropped lumber jolted through the small area and Burns's eyes flew open.

"What is that?"

"That, young man…" he pulled the covers from Burns "…is two women beginning to build the clinic."

"Women?"

Jacob laughed. "You going to let them put you to shame?"

For one second, Burns looked as if the idea was unacceptable, and then he settled back into the warm furs.

"They're so eager, let them do it."

Jacob nudged the boy with the toe of his boot. "Need I get a pitcher of water?" He was more than half-serious. The boy needed to learn responsibility. Maybe if Jacob had been able to have more influence on making Aaron be a man, his brother would still be alive. But his parents had always excused Aaron's behavior as exuberance. Jacob recognized it for what it was—irresponsibility. "You can choose to be a child and cuddle into your bed, or be a man and do some work." Words he wished he'd spoken to Aaron when he had the chance. Though, likely, Aaron would have scoffed at him.

Burns sat up and scowled at Jacob. "I'm a man." He scrambled to his feet and pushed out of the tent.

Relieved the boy had chosen work over sleep, Jacob checked on Donald, gave him some more laudanum then followed Burns outside, smiling when he saw the boy following Margie's orders and laughing at her teasing.

He walked around the proposed clinic, envisioning the modern facilities. At the corner of the lot he paused and studied the trail up the mountain. It was hard to believe men and women, even children, had scaled it in the midst of winter. He'd seen the upper portion up close, seen the way people had to bend over to keep from falling off. He'd seen, too, the things that suddenly had little importance when they had to be packed on a person's back up such an incline. So much stuff had been tossed aside that the place looked like a giant dump.

What must the natives think?

And yet Teena seemed eager to help.

Suspicion tugged at the back of his mind. Had she gone up the trail seeking injured people to practice her malarkey on? He thought of asking Margie and Frankie about her, but they had laughed like they shared some secret when he mentioned his concerns about the superstitious ways. Maybe he'd go find out for himself what she was up to.

"I'm going to see if anyone on the trail needs my help."

Frankie and Margie stopped work. They glanced at each other, then Margie nodded. "Sure. You go do that." Again, that darted look at her sister and the flicker of a smile between them. Then, as if sensing his curiosity about what they weren't saying, they bent and picked up some boards.

"I'll be back later." As he walked, a hundred questions burned in his brain. What did they know about Teena? Were there other shamans in the area? He had come here for one thing only: to build a clinic and establish adequate medical care. Then he would return to Seattle. Without getting involved in any complications.

* * *

Teena stood over the unconscious man. The trail was too rugged, too rocky for her to help him here. The man was too heavy for her to move. She needed help, but a glance to the side, where men and women marched upward, caring only about the promise of gold across the mountains, and she knew she would not find help from them. Mr. McIntyre promised God would never fail her. And the white man in the hut tucked into the trees, who carried the Good Book up and down the trail, reading it to others and praying with them and for them, promised the same thing.

Teena had stopped to visit him on her way up the trail. Thomas Stone was a kind man with a troubled soul. But he loved the Tlingit and the gold seekers equally. Perhaps it was God's love that made his heart so open to others. Thomas Stone had prayed with her when she told him about Dr. Jacob and her desire to learn the white man's healing ways. "Pray and trust God to open the door for you," Thomas Stone said. "God hears your prayers and answers as He deems best."

Well, if God heard the prayers of a Tlingit woman and did what was best, she could ask Him to send help for this injured man. *God, I need to get him where I can care for him. But I can't move him on my own. Please, send someone to help me.*

The stream of gold-hunting humans kept trudging by, unmindful or uncaring about the injured man. She perched on a rock and waited.

"Siteen." It was her Tlingit name, spoken by her

brother. God had sent help, and it was the best help she could ask for. Jimmy was strong as a papa bear. She sprang to her feet and clambered over the rocks to his side.

"I am glad to see you. I need someone to carry this man down the mountain."

Jimmy hesitated only a moment before he stepped off the trail, dropped to the ground the pack he carried and followed Teena to the injured man. He grunted as he heaved the man across his shoulders, then picked his way over the rocks toward Treasure Creek.

"I thought you would be helping the doctor," Jimmy said.

"He is not ready." Let Jimmy decide if she meant the building or something else.

"Remember what Father said. You cannot become a white woman."

Why did her family have such concerns? She had no desire to leave her native ways. "I only want to learn their healing ways. Besides, who would ever think I could be a white woman? Look at my eyes, my skin, my hair. I am native. Even if I wanted, I could not be anything else."

Jimmy made a noise in his throat that could be concern or doubt. "I don't want to see you searching for something that can't be yours."

"Do you mean learning from the doctor?" Had he heard Dr. Jacob's order to stay away?

"That. And more. These people are different than us, though some of their ways are interesting."

"Like what?"

"Reading. Don't you wish you could read from their books?"

"Yes. And I would like to read from Thomas Stone's Bible." She stopped so suddenly that Jimmy, following her, had to pull up hard.

"What's wrong?"

"Nothing." She forced her feet to continue onward. She told herself it didn't matter that Dr. Jacob climbed up the trail, yet her lungs had grown strangely tight and she was again aware of a quickening in the bottom of her heart. He hadn't yet seen them. Perhaps they could slip by unnoticed.

"I think 'nothing' is the doctor. Why do you care so much?"

"Because he is the answer to my prayer to learn their healing ways."

"Make sure that's all it is."

"What more could it be?"

Jimmy sighed. "He is a man, even if he is white. And you are a woman. If you weren't my sister I would say you are pretty, but I will only admit you aren't hard to look at. But who knows what the white man sees. How he feels about us."

She didn't respond, because she knew what he meant. Whites and natives liked different things, even in what they admired in the looks of each other.

Dr. Jacob glanced up and saw her. Their gazes crashed like waves against the sand during a high wind. Her heart pounded insistently. He was white. He didn't welcome her presence. Yet she saw nothing in his looks she disliked. It was more than the square shape of his face, the dark mystery of his eyes, the gouge in his chin. It was what she felt—his devotion to helping others, his trueness, his...

She couldn't explain it, but she knew, she just knew, he was a man who could be trusted, a man who would honor his word, a man who would love deeply.

She jerked her gaze away. Her father had already promised her to a man in the Wolf clan. Even if he hadn't, Dr. Jacob had already made his opinion of Teena clear, and the very things she admired in him made it impossible for him to change.

Yet he was the answer to her prayers. Somehow she must convince him to let her learn from him.

He stepped off the trail and climbed toward them.

"He is going to help?" Jimmy asked.

"He's a white doctor." She didn't say more. Dr. Jacob seemed to think the Tlingit could offer nothing to a white man's needs. A white doctor for the white man. Would he also think a native healer for natives? Would he help a native if the need arose?

He reached them, and ignoring Teena, went directly to Jimmy's side. "Let me examine this man."

Jimmy stood still but did not lower his burden. "I'm taking him off the mountain."

"Let me make sure he's not in danger of bleeding to death."

Jimmy and Teena exchanged amused looks. As if they would not attend to a wound before they moved the man. But Jimmy waited as Dr. Jacob lifted the man's eyelids and felt his head, then checked the rest of his body for wounds. He found nothing. Teena could have told him he wouldn't. She'd located only a lump on the back of the man's head.

"Could you carry him down to the clinic?"

At least he hadn't ordered Jimmy to do so. And Jimmy didn't ask where this clinic was. They all knew Dr. Jacob spoke more from hope than fact.

Jimmy agreed.

Dr. Jacob turned to Teena. "Is this your man?"

Teena giggled. "He is my brother, Jimmy."

Dr. Jacob nodded, somehow approving her answer, and reached out to shake hands with him.

Jimmy barely touched the man's outstretched hand then resumed his journey. Teena followed at his heels, Dr. Jacob close behind. She felt him with every breath, every thought. Somehow she had to convince him to teach her. Perhaps this would be her opportunity.

She fell back so she could speak without raising her voice. "You will need someone to watch him. I could do so." She allowed herself to meet his gaze briefly, before giving her attention back to the rocky path. But it was long enough to see a flash of possibility, and her heart swelled with hope.

"Would you promise not to use any native medicine?" He said the word in such a way she knew it must hurt him to say it.

"I have nothing to help a man who cannot wake up."

"That isn't what I asked."

She could not forsake the things she'd learned, the ways of nature that worked. He took her silence for what it was—refusal to agree to his conditions. "We can learn from each other."

"It cannot be." He clambered past her and followed on Jimmy's heels as they picked their way downward and reached the packed level path beside the town. A few minutes later, they reached the crowded lot that had been empty just two days ago.

"Bring him in here." Dr. Jacob lifted the tent flap. Jimmy ducked inside and lowered the injured man to the fur bedroll.

Teena followed and glanced around. Donald lay on a cot, his color good, his breathing easy. What did the doctor give for pain, if he wouldn't use the plants and herbs nature provided?

Dr. Jacob knelt beside the man from the trail as Jimmy stepped back. He lifted the eyelids again and pressed his fingers to the man's wrist.

Teena studied his every move, wondering why he did those things and wishing she dared ask. Perhaps if she remained quiet and motionless he would not notice her presence and give her another of those dismissive looks he'd given her earlier in the day.

Again, he pulled out the thing that fit into his ears and listened to the man's chest. "He seems fine, except for his unconsciousness."

Teena pressed back a desire to giggle. She could have told him all that. She sobered. Did he have a way to bring the man awake? All she knew to do was wait for nature to heal him or not.

"I'll watch him and wait for him to regain consciousness."

Teena swallowed back her disappointment. It seems the white man had no cure for this, either.

Dr. Jacob glanced at Donald, again pressed his fingers to the inside of the wrist, then he rose to his full height, brushing his head on the top of the tent and faced Jimmy. "Thanks for bringing him here." His gaze slid past Jimmy to Teena, and his gratitude shifted to disapproval. He didn't say a word, but his eyes signaled she wasn't welcome.

Silently, she backed from the tent.

Jimmy followed. "Why are you afraid of him? I thought he was meant to teach you their ways."

She met his hard gaze without flinching. "He does not know it yet." But if God could answer her prayer by sending the doctor, God would surely make the man agree to teach her.

Jimmy shook his head and strode back up the trail to retrieve his pack.

The Tucker sisters—the two who had not yet married and had vowed to never do so—nailed together walls for the new clinic. Teena moved closer. "Thought you were supposed to be working on the church. Didn't Mack decide it was time for a little room on top for a bell?"

Margie paused to answer Teena's question. "Mack decided this here clinic was more important. He gave us permission to leave the church work for the doctor. We don't care who pays us to work."

Frankie didn't stop adjusting the board, readying it to nail into place. "The doctor's young friend was helping, but he ran off two minutes after Jacob was out of sight. Ain't seen him since." She kicked the board into place. "About as bad as Lucy. Seems to me she runs off at the least little excuse."

Margie made a noisy sound. "Gotta make a meal for my man." The way she spoke told Teena she mimicked her sister.

Frankie kicked the board again unnecessarily. "You think the *man* could make himself a sandwich if he was hungry."

The pair looked as unhappy as twin bears perched on a beehive.

An idea sprouted and blossomed in Teena's busy brain. Dr. Jacob had ordered her to stay away from his patients, and he likely also meant the clinic. But the clinic was nothing more than an idea and hope right now. And if she assisted Margie and Frankie…well, surely he would see it was to his benefit. "I could help you."

Both Frankie and Margie stopped and stood like twin rocks. They stared at her, then shifted and considered each other. Margie turned back to Teena. "You know anything about building?"

"I've helped my father."

Again the sisters silently assessed each other,

as if wondering what experience helping her father constituted.

Margie nodded. "I 'spect you can do as well as any man. We accept."

"Thank you." She looked about her. What did they want her to do?

Margie didn't let her wait long to find out. "Grab that board and haul it over here, will you?"

Teena did as instructed, and in a few minutes was wielding a hammer and driving home nails. She giggled softly. Driving them home was perhaps a bit of exaggeration. She missed as often as she hit the nail.

Frankie let out a hearty laugh. "You'll catch on soon enough. Ain't nothing a woman can't learn to do, so far as I can tell."

Teena grabbed the hammer with both hands and aimed at the nail, giggling when she again missed.

Margie moved to her side. "Hold the hammer like so." She pulled Teena's hand lower on the handle. "Swing with your arm."

Teena did as instructed and soon had the nail in place. "There."

Margie chuckled. "You'll do just fine."

Teena felt Dr. Jacob's presence, and without turning, knew he had stepped from the tent. All the while she banged on the nail she'd been acutely aware of him. Between blows to the wood, she heard his murmurs as he dealt with the two injured men. But she dared not tiptoe closer to listen.

"Margie," he called, his voice soft but insistent. "May

I speak to you?" He tipped his head toward the other side of the tent, indicating she should join him there.

Margie didn't move. "Ain't nothing you need to say in private."

Dr. Jacob considered the three women, then nodded. "Very well." He cleared his throat. "I'm a medical doctor—"

"Yeah. We know."

He went on as if Margie hadn't interrupted him. "I believe in science. Superstition is not only ignorant but harmful."

Teena knew he meant her. Nevertheless, she stood her ground. Whether or not he liked it, and even if he denied it and fought against it, she was determined to learn his ways of healing. If that meant learning to hammer a nail and build a white man's house, she would do that, too. But she would not give up.

Margie and Frankie now stood side by side. "Say what you mean, Doc." It was obvious Margie spoke for both of them.

"I told you, I don't want a shaman near my patients."

Margie and Frankie dropped their tools and looked about ready to get mad.

Teena started to back away.

"You're not leaving." Margie's words stopped Teena's intended escape. Margie hadn't shifted her gaze from Dr. Jacob. "Seems to me, if you're interested in getting this here clinic built in a timely fashion, you can't be so all-fired concerned about who does the work. So long as it's getting done." Although her voice was low, Teena knew it held a load of anger.

She didn't dare breathe, feeling as if her life hung in the weight of Margie's deceptively soft words. Neither Margie nor Frankie moved, awaiting Dr. Jacob's decision. Teena knew the Tucker sisters well enough to know they would leave in the blink of an eye if Dr. Jacob pushed them the wrong way.

She watched the doctor as he assessed the sisters, knew he understood their silent ultimatum and was considering how to best deal with it.

When Jacob sucked in air like a drowning man rescued from the waters, she knew he realized his limited options. "I have no problem with her helping you."

He gently emphasized the word *you,* making it clear she could help them but not him. His words clawed into the secret depths of her heart.

Ignoring the way her eyes stung, she picked up another nail and pounded it into place. When she finished and glanced to where Dr. Jacob had stood, he was gone, and Margie and Frankie were busy measuring a board.

Chapter Three

Jacob strode toward the waterfront, as if he needed to put out a fire. Anger burned through his veins. He fought for control. He did not want a shaman hanging about his clinic. If his brother had received real medical help he would likely be alive still.

Jacob had tried to convince Aaron not to go north seeking gold, but once Aaron made up his mind to do something he refused to listen to reason. He'd been the same since he was a child.

He searched through the crowds. Where was Burns? He'd agreed to help with the construction of the clinic, though it wasn't the building he was concerned about as much as Burns's safety.

He went as far as the beginning of the trail without a sign of Burns. Surely the boy wouldn't head up there on his own.

Jacob sighed. The boy would do anything that entered his mind, without regard for the consequences. If only Jacob could instill a little sense of responsibility in him before he made a foolish decision. He realized his desire sprang not only out of concern about Burns, but also from a wish that he could have prevented Aaron from a choice that lead ultimately to his death.

He spun on his heel and took a slightly different route, hoping to locate Burns among the throng, but he passed the place he'd started without any sign of the boy. He pressed onward. Again he reached the end of the beach, and saw a trail leading through the trees and followed it. A few hundred yards later, the path opened to a clearing with several wooden structures, each with a narrow, low door but no windows. Smoke drifted from one building.

The place was quiet. Peaceful. No gold seekers here. A movement caught his attention. A man sat in the sunshine, a basketlike hat on his head. The man was an elderly native. Was this where Teena's family lived? It suited her. He could imagine her quiet and serene in this setting. Nothing seemed to ruffle her. Not even his rudeness. He considered himself a gentle, refined man, and yet something about her brought from him harsh, unkind words. It didn't make sense.

Suddenly, he realized his patients were alone while he stared at an old man rocking in the sunshine. He turned and rushed back through the crowds, seeing nothing of Burns as he trotted to the clinic. Already the walls began to take shape. The three women worked side by side. Margie turned to Teena and laughed.

He slowed momentarily, wishing he knew what Teena said. Then he dismissed such foolishness and hurried on.

He didn't notice Burns until he reached the boardwalk. The boy sat cross-legged on the ground, playing with a pup. When he saw Jacob he jumped up, clutching the pup in his arms.

"Look what I got."

Jacob jerked to a stop. "A dog?"

"Some man gave it to me. Said he didn't want to drag around a useless pup. Isn't he sweet?" Burns scrubbed the animal's ears and gave Jacob pleading eyes.

Aaron had once dragged home a sorry-looking pup and begged to keep it. He'd spent hours with the animal, but it wasn't healthy, and died despite everyone's efforts. Aaron had cried. He'd cursed God when Mother and Father couldn't hear him. Said it was unfair. Jacob had been powerless to help either the sick pup or his heartbroken brother.

"He looks like he'd grow to the size of a horse. I think you'd better take him back." His words, fueled by a thousand regrets and a lifetime of sorrow over his brother, were harsher than he intended.

Burns drew back. The three women stopped work to watch the proceedings.

"I aim to keep him. I'll move to the beach if you won't have him here."

Jacob could not imagine how the boy would survive out there. In about two days he would be starving, and if anything like Aaron, too proud to admit his mistake. "Who will feed him? And you?"

Burns's expression revealed his worry about food. After all, food, and plenty of it, were essential for growing boys and…Jacob sighed…and growing dogs. He didn't want to do anything he'd live to regret, and he knew if he allowed Burns to stalk off in anger, he would regret it in the depths of his soul. He examined the pup. He'd at least make sure it was healthy before he gave his verdict. The pup's fur was silky and thick. It glistened, indicating he'd been fed a good diet. Jacob lifted the pup's lips and examined his mouth. The pup wriggled eagerly and tried to lick his hands. "He seems in good health." The last thing he wanted was to watch another young man put through the pain of losing a pet. "I'll make you a deal." This was an opportunity to help the boy learn a little responsibility.

Burns brightened.

"I'll let you keep the dog here on one condition."

"I'll do anything. Just name it."

Burns had already agreed to work on the clinic, but seemed to have forgotten. Perhaps this would add a needed incentive to get him more involved. "Work on the clinic as you agreed."

Burns nodded. "Then he can stay?"

"I would expect you to work hard. Help build the clinic and give me a hand with the patients."

Burns looked agreeable until Jacob mentioned the patients. "I ain't never taken care of a sick person." He sounded like he'd as soon starve to death.

"I will teach you." He recalled Teena's desire that he teach her. He tried not to glance at her, but couldn't stop himself. Would she resent his offer to Burns? But she studied the ground and he couldn't see her expression. For some reason, he wished things could be different. However, there was no way of changing the facts. What she wanted was impossible. She had no education. Likely couldn't read. Trusted superstition rather than science for treatment, clung to her old ways. He forced his attention back to Burns. "Is it a deal?"

Burns nodded. "Deal."

"Fine. Then tie the pup and come help me."

Burns found a bit of rope and tied the pup to a stake. He spent considerable time patting the animal and reassuring it. If he gave Jacob's patients half the attention he gave the dog, Jacob would have no cause for complaint.

He didn't wait for Burns to finish with his pet, but ducked inside. Donald had rolled to his side, obviously feeling less pain. Good news there.

The other man breathed regularly but showed no sign of opening his eyes.

Jacob had finished his examination by the time Burns entered. As he explained what he expected from the boy, he heard the women talking as they worked. He couldn't make out their words but recognized Teena's musical, soft voice, a marked contrast to the heavier, heartier tones of the Tucker sisters.

He forced his mind back to the task of showing

Burns how to check each man and care for any pressing personal needs.

Burns nodded, eager to earn the right to keep the dog, but shrinking back at the idea of touching either of the men.

Jacob tried to reassure him. "It's only when I need to be away." He would hang out a shingle today. People would realize they could come to him, but he would still have to tend to the sick and injured in their makeshift homes and on the trail.

"I'm going to name him *Yukon*. After the gold field."

Jacob knew then and there that the dog would get more attention than any patients.

"I'm going to teach him all kinds of tricks."

"Teach him to obey your commands. It's the only way to keep him safe."

Burns considered the suggestion. "Right. He will learn to sit, stay and follow. He'll be a good dog." He threw an arm across Jacob's shoulders in an awkward hug. "You won't be sorry. I promise." The boy stepped back, embarrassed by his show of affection. "Can I go now?"

Jacob nodded. Burns dashed out. Jacob heard him talking to the dog and scrubbed at his chin. He was glad to be able to have a small part in bringing some happiness to the boy. From what Burns had told him, he knew the boy had lost his mother a number of years ago, and his father was cruel and neglectful. No wonder he was anxious to get to the gold fields. Jacob understood the hunt for gold was of minor importance to Burns. Escape was the foremost reason for the trip to Treasure Creek.

Teena's soft voice reached him and Burns answered. He strained to hear what they said but couldn't make it out. He tried to decide if he minded Burns and Teena striking up a friendship; he found he minded, but his reason didn't make sense. He didn't feel lonely. Didn't wish he could enjoy a friendship with…

With a muttered sound of disgust he turned his attention back to his patients. He was here only to establish adequate medical care. Nothing more.

The next morning, he rose from his crowded quarters to the welcome noise of building. Somehow the pup had made it indoors and curled up beside Burns.

"Burns."

The boy jerked to a sitting position, guilt flooding his gaze. "He was crying. He's not used to being alone." He wrapped a protective arm about the pup and received a generous licking.

Jacob struggled to contain his amusement at the eager affection between the two. But he must bear in mind his responsibility to his patients. "Nevertheless, this is a hospital for now, and animals aren't allowed."

Burns scrambled to his feet. "Come on, Yukon. Let's go outside."

Jacob wanted to call the pair back. Tell them to make themselves at home. Instead, he turned to the uncon-

wish he was, though. He cares about me more than my father does. Ain't got no brother."

That one statement—*I wish he was*—sat like something warm and sweet in the secret corner of her heart. A man who won the respect of someone younger deserved admiration.

Even if he saved his kindness for the white man.

She sighed. Life used to be so simple. So straightforward. She knew what was expected of her—work hard to feed the family, respect her elders, marry the man of her father's choosing, follow the events of each season. But things had changed.

She brought her attention back to the trail. This hungry search for gold had turned her life upside down, shifted her world sideways. Things would never be the same.

As if her thoughts had brought him toward her, Dr. Jacob climbed the path. He didn't look her way. She wondered that the silent cry of her soul at seeing him didn't draw his attention to her. Who was this man? Why should she feel such a stirring inside at the mere sight of him?

She didn't move. Barely breathed. She wanted him to see her. But hoped he wouldn't. She was not in a mood to deal with the way his eyes alternately flashed disapproval then darkened with some kind of interest. Or was it curiosity?

He passed out of sight.

She sat there a moment or two, waiting for her insides to calm, her reason to return. Then she pushed to her feet and headed down the trail to help with the clinic construction.

The three Tucker sisters were hard at work in the afternoon sun when she reached the clinic. Perhaps they no longer needed her help. She hung back to watch and wait.

"Burns," Frankie called. "I could use a hand with this here board." The boy hurriedly left his pup.

As Lucy waited for Burns to do Frankie's bidding, she pulled out a pretty white hankie from her pocket and patted her brow. Both her sisters stared.

"What?" Lucy demanded.

"What good's that little bit of cloth?" Frankie appointed herself spokeswoman. "Where's your bandanna?"

"I gave it to Caleb."

"Why?" Both her sisters looked her up and down like she had suddenly changed form before their eyes.

"Well, for goodness' sake. Can't a woman give her man a gift?" She jammed the hankie back in her pocket and picked up a hammer to drive a nail into a board with such fury that Teena flinched.

Burns stared wide-eyed. He glanced over his shoulder, as if wondering how to escape these rowdy women.

Margie and Frankie considered each other then shrugged, gave a sad shake to their heads and returned to work.

"You want to help me, Teena?" Margie gave Lucy a sideways look.

Teena worked alongside Margie for some time. "You remind me of a friend I used to have," Teena said, after the tension had melted away.

Margie removed nails she held in her mouth to ask, "A good one, I hope?"

"Sarah McIntyre. Her father taught us about Jesus." As they worked together, she told Margie about the white friend she'd had as a child.

"Sounds like she accepted you the way you are."

Teena considered the words. "She never saw me as an Indian, but as a friend. I never saw her as white, but a friend."

"That's special. Not often we find such acceptance. I can tell you, not everyone sees past the rough exterior of the Tucker sisters to our hearts." Margie shook her head. "I never figured any of us would marry. I don't aim to give up my independence for the sake of a man." She gave Lucy a sideways look, but Lucy either didn't hear or decided to act as if she hadn't. "How 'bout you, Frankie?"

"Not me either." Frankie puffed out her lips and made a rumbling noise. "I got bigger aspirations."

Teena wondered what those aspirations were, but she didn't have the right to ask.

Apparently, Margie thought she did. "You still hankering for a man's job?"

"Ain't no man's job I couldn't do," Frankie muttered, her shoulders rigid.

Lucy stopped work. "It's not about proving you're

equal to a man. It's about sharing—" She patted her chest then jerked her eyes downward and stopped speaking.

Teena waited, wanting to know what made Lucy smile like she had a special secret, but Lucy didn't continue. Instead, she set her hammer on a stack of wood.

"I'm going home to make supper for Caleb."

Frankie and Margie both stared after her departing figure. "Well, if that don't beat all," Frankie mumbled, then resumed work.

Teena and Margie did the same, the unnatural silence broken by hammer beats. For Teena's part, she longed to ask Lucy if being married to Caleb brought that sweet smile to her lips.

"Anyone there," one of the men in the tent called out.

"Guess he's calling you," Frankie said to Burns.

"I don't know what to do for them." The boy looked scared half to death.

Teena itched to step inside and offer her comfort, but she feared Jacob's anger. Feared triggering it would end forever any hope of being allowed to learn from him. However, Burns's discomfort was very real. "Just ask what he wants. Perhaps only a cup of water."

Burns's eyes were wide as he ducked into the tent. Teena listened from outside. If she was needed she would disregard Dr. Jacob's order to stay away from his patients. Not even to please him would she ignore a person's sufferings. Not even a white man's.

Burns stepped out in a few minutes. "Donald wanted

a drink just like you said." He glanced at the trail. "I wish Jacob would get back. The other man opened his eyes and stared at me." He shivered. "It gives me the creeps."

Teena knew of a ground root that would ease the man's worry as he recovered his mind, but she dared not give it to him. Perhaps she could make a tea using it, and ask Burns to get the man to sip it. She took a step toward her sack of remedies.

"Here comes Jacob," Burns yelled. "Hurry up. That man is waking up."

Teena slid back to Margie's side and pretended an interest she didn't feel at the position of a board.

Margie considered her. "You want to help, don't you?"

"I want to learn."

"He will come around. He'll soon 'nough see that you can't judge a person by the outside."

Teena wished she could believe it was so.

She edged closer to the tent to listen to the conversation inside. She heard Dr. Jacob murmur to the patients but she could not tell what he did. She closed her eyes and imagined him touching the men's wrists, pressing that little instrument to their chests. Why did he do those things? What did he learn about illness in doing so? What did he give Donald for pain? Did it work better than what she used? Why?

Margie and Frankie hammered away at the rising walls. The noise made it impossible for Teena to hear Dr. Jacob. *God, the Creator, Mr. McIntyre said You would listen to me, even if I am a Tlingit. Hear my prayer. Let me learn from this man.* Would He truly listen to a Tlingit woman—a superstitious healer, as Dr. Jacob described her?

"Burns," the doctor called. "I need your help."

Burns reluctantly ducked inside as Teena watched in longing frustration.

A few minutes later, the tent flap parted and Dr. Jacob and Burns shuffled out, the man who had lain without moving between them. He blinked in the sunshine and drew in a long breath, then murmured, "The sun feels good."

Dr. Jacob settled him against a roll of canvas and handed him a cup of water. "Can you tell us your name?"

"Name's Emery Adams." He sounded weary, but at least he knew his name.

Teena slid a happy glance toward Jacob and caught her breath at the look he gave her. "It is good he knows his name," she murmured.

"It is very good." His gaze held hers, silently rejoicing. She couldn't force her eyes away. Couldn't think of anything but the shared gladness of this good news. At that precise moment, something happened she was at a loss to explain—a connection she'd never felt with anyone else, a spiritual experience almost as profound as when Mr. McIntyre told her about Jesus.

She would never again feel the same inside.

Jacob turned away first. "How did you injure yourself?"

Emery snorted a bitter laugh and grabbed at his head. "Oh, it hurts."

Jacob touched the man's shoulder. "Take it easy."

Emery closed his eyes a moment. "I was attacked. Someone sneaked up and hit me. I heard them coming. Guessed what they had in mind but didn't have time to defend myself." He glanced about. "Don't suppose you found any of my belongings with me?"

"I didn't find you." Jacob didn't look toward Teena for two heartbeats. "This woman did." He nodded toward her. "Did he have anything with him?"

She stepped forward and faced the man. "Nothing."

Emery's eyes narrowed. "'Course not. Indians believe in finders keepers. No respect for a man's belongings."

Teena felt his dislike of her. Knew it was based on her being a Tlingit and no other reason. Little did he understand that a Tlingit's honor would never allow them to touch the belongings of another.

Nor would there be thanks from this man. Not even for saving his life. She moved away, out of his sight.

Frankie edged closer. "Did you get a look at your attackers?"

"'Fraid not."

"Can you remember anything at all? A word? Their boots? Anything at all?"

Emery squinted. "I seem to remember one of them saying Harmon. I don't know if it's a name or what."

Frankie squatted to eye level with Emery. "Can you

describe any of your belongings? Something that makes them unique?"

Emery patted his vest pocket. "My watch. It was a gift from my father." He described it.

"Good. That's something to go on." Frankie stood. "I'll trot on over to the sheriff's office and let him know."

She returned shortly with Sheriff Ed Parker, who made a few notes.

"I'll pass the information along. Someone will likely spot the watch. We'll do our best to find it and the men who robbed you." He touched the brim of his hat and left.

"That's enough for one day. It's time to get you back to bed." Jacob signaled to Burns and they helped the man back into the tent.

Teena and the Tuckers returned to work.

Teena knew the moment Jacob stepped out of the tent, even though she couldn't see him. She didn't need to. Her heart felt him with every beat.

He poked his head around the wall she worked on.

The hammer hung in midair—halfway between her nose and a nail she intended to pound. But she couldn't move. He was too close. And he watched her.

"I'm sorry," he murmured. "Emery had no right to accuse you of stealing. Please forgive him."

Her gaze sought his. He looked so regretful it stung her heart.

"It's not your fault. Why should you be sorry?"

He shrugged and gave a crooked smile that melted

every remnant of resentment at Emery's accusations. "I just feel I should apologize for his behavior."

His smile widened and the inside of her head felt washed with honey. "Apology accepted." She knew her smile was as wide as his.

Suddenly his lips flattened, his expression darkened and he turned away.

She hit the nail as hard as she could.

He might apologize for others, but it didn't change how he viewed her. Why did she think it would?

Chapter Four

"Doctor Calloway?"

Jacob looked through his supplies, itching to arrange them properly on shelves. He turned toward the man calling his name… Mack Tanner with a woman and young child at his side. Jacob strode over to greet them. "About time you came to check on things."

"I'm not here to—"

The woman laughed daintily. "Of course you are. Everyone knows how you have to make sure the whole town is run according to your guidelines." She leaned closer to Jacob to murmur, "It keeps him far too busy trying to run the town and be preacher, too. If only he could find a preacher—persuade Thomas Stone to take the job—he could spend a little more time at home with us."

Mack looked like he might argue, then grinned. "Jacob, meet my wife, Lana. I'm afraid she understands me too well for me to be able to hide my true motivation." He scooped up the little boy. "This is our son, Georgie."

The Tuckers had been working on the far wall of the building and hustled around to greet the visitors.

Jacob waited, wondering why Teena hadn't come, as well.

Frankie clapped her hands. "Well, lookee here. A little man come to visit."

Georgie tried to escape Mack's arms.

"Hang on a minute." Mack lowered the boy, his feet scrambling for motion long before he hit dirt.

Georgie ran as fast as his short, unsteady legs would carry him toward the Tucker sisters. "Cookie?"

Margie scooped him up and tousled his hair. "No cookies here. You'll have to come visit us at home for one."

"I brought a cake," Lana said, holding out a basket. "A welcome gift for the good doctor."

Jacob took it to his makeshift table. "Can I offer you tea?"

"A tea party." Frankie clapped her hands. "I love a good ol' tea party." She hesitated. "We *are* invited, aren't we?"

Jacob answered. "Of course. Everyone is. Make yourselves comfortable." He waved around to the assortment of "chairs"—two short stools, a taller one, several chunks of log standing on end and another, longer, one laid lengthwise. As the assorted crew settled, Jacob filled the kettle and set it on his tiny portable stove.

From experience, he knew it would take a good long while to boil. Hopefully no one would mind.

"Glad the building is coming along," Mack said. "We'll soon have the bell and stained-glass windows for the church. I'm expecting them to arrive any day." He glanced toward the harbor. "Maybe on the next boat. I'd like to see the construction complete by the time it gets here."

The Tucker sisters talked at once and Lana tried to insert a comment.

Mack held up his hand to silence them. "I know there's lots of work to do yet. But with the sawmill now operating, it's easier to get construction done." He sat back, a dreamy look on his face.

Lana gave him an affectionate yet accusing look. "As if you didn't have enough work without starting a sawmill."

Mack patted her hand. "It's important to get things done speedily. Once the steeple is done, people will see the church as soon as they venture into the harbor." He brought his gaze back to those around him and Jacob was struck by the determination he saw. "They will understand what this town stands for." He squeezed Lana's hand. "Soon people will learn the *real* treasure isn't up the trail or buried around town, but in knowing and obeying God."

Jacob looked from one to the other. "Real treasure? What's this all about?"

Frankie shrugged. "According to the legend, a Russian czar buried sixty nuggets of gold somewhere out here. Thomas Stone found six nuggets. People don't believe he found all the treasure. They aren't going to stop looking until they find it all."

Mack sighed heavily. "It's nothing but gossip and speculation that there is a buried treasure in the vicinity. They speculate I have a fortune hidden somewhere. In part because I have no use for bankers."

Jacob wondered at the way Mack glanced at Lucy.

"The rumors of gold almost cost me Lana. Some scoundrel out to find my gold threatened her and injured her in the hopes they could force her to reveal the hiding place." He pulled her close. "I decided then and there to dispose of my gold. I bought land with it. I'm convinced gold is a curse."

Lana nuzzled against his shoulder. "Money doesn't have to be the cause of evil. It can be used for good."

"But when I think how you were hurt—"

Lana pressed her fingers to Mack's mouth to stop him from saying more.

Something besides the idea of gold interested Jacob. Mack said Lana was injured. "Has your wife recovered from her attack? Were her injuries tended to?"

"I'm fine. All I got was a little cut behind my ear."

Mack tightened his arm about his wife. "You were knocked out."

"I got excellent care."

"You saw a doctor?" Jacob thought he was the first doctor in the area.

She chuckled softly. "Not exactly. Teena Crow

tended me. Her medicine is responsible for my quick recovery."

Jacob sat back, stunned that this well-educated woman would believe the Indian drivel had any value.

Lana glanced around. "Where is Teena? I thought she was helping here."

"Yup. She is." In unison, the Tuckers bellowed out her name. "Teena." As an afterthought, Margie added, "Someone here to see you."

Teena eased around the corner of the building, her gaze slipping from Lana to Mack to Jacob.

He felt her caution across the few feet between them. She'd been hurt by Emery's unkind words. How many times had she endured similar comments and a hateful attitude? He wished he could assure her not everyone thought that way about the Tlingit. Not everyone judged her by her race. His jaw tightened. Yet some aspects of her lifestyle needed to be eradicated. Ignorance and superstition had no place in medical care.

"Teena, please join us." He thought of how they'd silently rejoiced together when Emery was able to recall his name and the details of his accident. There was something in their shared look that he wished he could claim for his own.

Teena hesitated, then slowly edged toward the circle. She chose an upright log a few feet beyond the others.

"I brought cake," Lana said, offering Teena a piece.

Teena seemed about to refuse, then took it and murmured her thanks.

Jacob noticed she did not take a bite.

"I never got a chance to properly thank you for rescuing me and taking care of my injuries." Lana spoke slowly, as if her throat tightened. "I acted badly that day. I thought you meant to harm me. I apologize for my behavior and thank you from the bottom of my heart."

"I thank you, too." Mack's voice thickened with emotion.

With her head downturned, her braids hanging over her shoulders on each side, Jacob could not guess at Teena's reaction. Slowly she lifted her face, her expression serene, gentle. "I only did what I must do."

Continuing caution lingered in her eyes and he understood she had learned to be guarded around white people.

Mack cleared his throat. "Back to the clinic. How soon do you think you'll be done?"

Jacob let Frankie answer the question. "It's going well. I could return to the church building and Margie could stay here and work. She has Teena and Burns to help. Maybe Lucy could help me."

Lucy narrowed her eyes. "Of course I'll help."

Jacob wondered what undercurrents raced beneath the words they spoke.

Mack nodded. "Might be a good idea."

Jacob glanced around. "Where's Burns? It's not like him to miss out on cake." A short time ago he and Yukon had run around the piles of lumber and the crates cluttering the ground.

Teena suddenly exhibited a great interest in the shape of her piece of cake. Frankie and Margie played with

Georgie, tickling him and making him laugh. Lucy picked the last crumbs of cake from her plate.

"Is there something I should know?" Jacob demanded.

Frankie faced him. "Nothing to concern yourself with. Yukon was hungry, so we told him to go fishing."

Jacob lifted his hands in a helpless gesture. "How will the boy ever learn responsibility if he's allowed to leave his work whenever he wants?"

Margie grinned at him. "Feeding his dog is being responsible, don't you think?"

He knew he fought a lost cause and turned back to Mack. "I really need a nurse, or someone interested in learning to be one."

The air filled with tension so thick he could have cut it and packaged it. He didn't miss the glance Lana and Mack exchanged, and was equally aware of the exasperation the Tucker sisters wore broadly on their faces. No one looked at Teena, but he guessed they all wondered why he refused to take her under his wing.

Because his patients shouldn't fear they might be getting as much home remedies as science. A tiny voice niggled at the back of his mind. How did she treat Lana so she had no ill aftereffects? Just random good fortune?

Another, less well-defined reason drove his decision to not have her work with him. Something about her made him aware of his deficiencies. He'd tried all his life to live up to a certain code of conduct—obey

God, honor his father and mother, seek the good of others. Yes, he often failed. His best efforts but dust. He didn't need anything or anyone to remind him, and Teena, with her gentle goodness, did. "I don't suppose you know of a person who would fill the bill?"

Mack considered the question. "Can't say as I do, but I'll ask around. You never know who might be interested."

"I'd appreciate if you would. There's one more thing that needs to be addressed. This town—"

Mack's eyebrows jerked skyward, as if surprised anyone could find fault with his town.

"This place is ripe for an epidemic." Jacob waved toward the waterfront crowded with people and goods. "Inadequate sanitation. Unsanitary water supplies. I'm surprised there hasn't been an outbreak of cholera or—" He shook his head unwilling to voice the extent of his concern.

"What do you suggest we do?"

"Build latrines toward the trees. Insist people use them. Fine those who don't. And dig some water wells. The creek is almost certainly contaminated."

Mack nodded. "I'll see to it as soon as I get a chance."

Georgie squirmed away from Margie and went to lean against his mother's knees.

"Mack, we should go. Georgie is getting tired."

"Of course." Mack stood and scooped up the boy. "I expect we'll see you all in church Sunday. Everyone attends."

Jacob understood it was an order as much as invitation and guessed Mack was used to having his orders obeyed in his town. Not that Jacob intended to miss the service. He couldn't afford to do anything to displease God.

Jacob and Burns crossed the street to the church. For the past two days, he'd heard the sound of sawing and pounding from this area that rivaled the sound at the clinic as the two Tucker sisters worked at the building. Today, Sunday, it was quiet. He could see boards cut in matching lengths. "Looks like they're going to put in a walkway here."

"You sure Yukon is going to be okay by himself?"

"Emery is there if he needs anything, but he's got water and a bone to chew. I think he'll manage on his own for an hour or so."

"I don't like Emery."

"Takes all kinds to make the world." He hadn't much liked the man since his cruel words to Teena.

Emery's headaches were less frequent every day. Tomorrow, Jacob would tell the man he could go. It kind of surprised him he hadn't left on his own accord already. Instead, he hung about asking questions, stopping passersby to talk to them.

Jacob didn't care for the man's curiosity about Mack and Lana, especially when every time Jacob drew close, Emery stopped talking as if he had a secret. A couple of times Jacob caught the words *gold* and *treasure*. Of course Emery had overheard Mack telling about buried

gold. Too bad he hadn't listened to the whole story—
that it was gone.

Or was it? He'd heard such conflicting stories over
the past few days, it was impossible to guess what was
true and what was conjecture. One thing for certain,
people were set on finding the nuggets. He'd heard
more. Stuff that disturbed him. People said Mack and
his partner, Jed, had hit pay dirt. Jed had died soon
after, leaving Lana a widow with a young son.

"Seems between the two of them, they must have a
fortune in gold." He'd listened to a pair discuss it as he
ate breakfast at the café. "Mack don't make no secret
about not trusting banks. Where you think they keep
their gold?"

The pair had talked about various possibilities, including inside the Tanner house. Jacob could not walk
away without speaking up.

"There is no Tanner treasure. He bought land with
his money. Believes land is a good investment."

The pair had laughed uproariously, joined in by
others who listened freely.

"Only a fool would buy worthless land, and Tanner
ain't no fool."

Jacob knew it was useless to argue further. But it
bothered him that men lost all sense of reasonableness
when it came to gold.

They reached the church and stepped into the log
structure, with its floor of split logs and backless pun-
cheons as benches. He chose a seat halfway up. He'd

have preferred to sit at the back but feared it might indicate he wasn't as religious as he ought to be. Within minutes he was crowded on each side. Every bench was full to overflowing.

He stole a glance about. Margie and Frankie had donned clean overalls in honor of the occasion. Behind them, Lucy, wearing a fetching dress, sat beside her husband he recognized as Caleb Johnson, the harbormaster. The benches close to the door were crowded with Tlingit Indians. Teena sat on one side of an older man, her brother, Jimmy, on the other. Teena met his gaze, held it unblinkingly. He saw the clear challenge in her eyes. As if she demanded why he should be surprised to see her and others of her clan in church. He jerked back to face forward. He truly hadn't expected them. Yes, he'd heard most of them had converted. It just hadn't entered his head they would worship in the same building. He couldn't explain to himself why he hadn't considered it. Guilt churned up his insides. Was he prejudiced? Would God punish him even though it was unintentional?

Mack stood at the front and wished the congregation a blessed Sunday. He led them in a few hymns. Jacob smiled with enjoyment as they sang without accompaniment, a blend of soprano, baritone and monotone voices. It was so natural and unconstrained.

"Our scripture reading for today," Mack said, "is Hebrews, chapter eleven, verse six. 'But without faith it is impossible to please Him; for he that cometh to God must believe that He is, and that He is a rewarder of them that diligently seek Him.'" He closed the Bible and leaned forward. "Too often, I fear, we think God rewards us for our efforts rather than our faith. Faith is simply believing in God's love and goodness. Not our own efforts."

Jacob squirmed. Did he have enough faith? If receiving God's favor indicated so, then he would conclude he did not. Otherwise, wouldn't Aaron still be alive? His mother recovered instead of gone? How did one produce more faith? He didn't know, and although he listened to every word Mack spoke, all the man said was faith is trusting God. It didn't help Jacob's quandary one bit.

The service ended and the crowd filed out—a slow, tedious exodus. He finally stepped into the sunshine and glimpsed Teena as she hurried away with her family. He overheard murmurs from a few who thought the Tlingit should worship in their village. The realization of his own prejudice—unintentional as it was—made him realize he must do something to correct it.

"Teena."

She stopped and turned, murmured something to Jimmy, who nodded and took the older man onward.

Jacob closed the distance between them in long strides. "It was nice to see you."

"You see me every day." Her smile teased dark lights into the irises of her eyes. He found it difficult to think as they flashed.

"I suppose I do." The sun warmed his back, highlighted the strong features of her face. "Somehow it's different."

Her smile softened. "Perhaps seeing me in church makes it possible for you to see I am not controlled by ignorant superstitions."

Her words stung his conscience. "I don't mean to be unkind."

"I know. I understand that you think our ways are too far apart for us to bridge the distance, but I pray God will make a way to do so. My people need your kind of medicine."

He hoped she meant she would abandon her ways in favor of modern medicine.

She nodded, her eyes full of dark mystery. "Perhaps you can learn from our ways, too."

Her words drove away the hope he'd allowed himself, but before he could think of a defense, she glided away after the rest of her clan.

Jacob took a break from cleaning his instruments. His shingle hung on a post. The clinic was steadily taking shape. Soon the outside walls would be complete. The inside would take several more days, and then he'd move his practice into proper facilities. He could hardly wait.

He'd had a number of patients over the past few days—dog bites, insect bites, knife cuts, a couple of broken limbs plus several cases of bowel upset from eating improperly. Nothing as serious as Donald, who was well on his way to recovery.

Emery had reluctantly left on Monday, which raised suspicious questions in Jacob's mind. Why was he so eager to hang around? He'd asked Jacob about Mack's buried gold, but all Jacob knew was what the man had already overheard. "He says there is no gold."

"Likely he's lying to protect it."

"Mack strikes me as an honest man. Not one given to lying."

Emery had snorted at that. "Doc, you hang around here long and you'll discover men are willing to sell their souls for gold."

Jacob didn't care for the man's attitude about Mack. Emery was also prejudiced against Teena in a most shocking way. Whenever he saw her he would say something disparaging about Indians.

Jacob wasn't sorry he finally left.

He placed his instruments in a metal tray, filled it with water and set it on his portable stove to boil. He'd be doubly glad for a proper stove.

He sighed. He hated the primitive conditions. The crowding. The mud. The rain. The bugs. As soon as he had the clinic properly set up he would advertise for a doctor to run it. He could hardly wait to return to his practice in Seattle, his promise to his mother fulfilled.

Burns was still the only help with the patients he had, and he was not exactly eager for the job. Despite Mack's inquiries, he'd located no one interested in helping him as a nurse. Like Mack had said, most people were far more interested in what lay over the Chilkoot Trail.

He couldn't see Margie and Teena, but he heard the murmur of their conversation as they began the day's work. Frankie and Lucy had returned to work on the church. Mack was as eager to have everything ready for the arrival of the bell as Jacob was to have his clinic completed.

The pair came around the partially constructed clinic and set about measuring and building a door.

"Doc, we'll start on the inside. Won't take long." Margie liked to converse as she worked.

Teena said little, but seemed to see everything.

Jacob would be glad when they finished. Certainly he looked forward to better surroundings, but also it meant Teena would no longer be only a few feet away at any given time. He was acutely conscious of her exact whereabouts, even though he vowed he wouldn't pay attention.

Like now. Without looking, he knew she had gone inside the clinic to hold a board for Margie.

"Are you the new doctor?"

He turned toward the sweet, refined voice. A beautiful young woman, dressed in a stylish gown and holding a parasol to protect her face, regarded him from the boardwalk. "Yes. I'm Dr. Calloway. What can I do for you?"

"I heard you were looking for someone to help." She smiled sweetly, widening her blue eyes as she did. Her fair hair was curled and pinned up in an attractive fashion. None of which mattered if she had come to assist him.

"That's correct." If this woman was a nurse, she would be a gift from God.

"I have no experience, but I'd be glad to help and willing to learn."

Jacob restrained his profound joy. He must have done something right to be favored by such an offer. "You are an answer to prayer."

She ducked her head shyly.

"When can you start? And what's your name?"

"Oh, my. I'm so sorry. Forgive my lapse. Annabelle Dubois. I came on the recent boat. I'm living in the boardinghouse for now. I can begin immediately if you so desire." She favored him with a blazing smile.

"Good. Good. Come along. I'll introduce you to my patient and show you my temporary set-up." He indicated she should follow him. "This will be the clinic when it's finished."

She glanced inside and nodded.

Teena stood holding a piece of wood, her eyes dark and accusing.

No reason he should feel he'd done something wrong. From the beginning, he'd been clear he couldn't accept Teena as a nurse unless she abandoned her native practices. Imagine a shaman nurse. But he failed to smile at the idea.

Annabelle noticed Teena and backed away, her eyes wide with either fright or dislike.

Jacob would have ignored the tension, but good manners dictated he introduce everyone, including Teena.

Teena murmured a quick greeting and slid away as silent as a shadow.

Margie, however, did not do the same. "You gonna

help the doc?" She ran her gaze up and down the woman, taking in the fine gown and spotless shoes. She stopped at the pretty white gloves. "Bet you never had dirty hands in your life."

Annabelle smiled gently. "I've come North for a change. I will do whatever I need."

"Humph." Margie grabbed a board and swung it in an arc that would have caught Annabelle in the stomach had Jacob not pulled her out of the way.

"Oh, my." Annabelle's tiny hand rested on his forearm as he steadied her.

He stepped aside as soon as she recovered her balance. "Until the clinic is ready, I am caring for patients in the tent or out in the open. As you can imagine, it is far from ideal." The water covering his instruments boiled and he moved the pan to the edge of the stovetop to simmer. "The instruments need to be boiled after every use. I'll show you how to clean them and sterilize them."

"How exciting."

No doubt she would soon enough find the job tedious. "I only have one patient right now. Come and meet him." He held the tent flap open and let her precede him. She stepped inside and pressed a dainty hanky to her nose.

He sniffed. Perhaps he'd grown used to the odor of wet clothes and sweaty socks. Not to mention the wild smell from the furs. He sifted through the scents. Only one would concern him—the smell of infection from Donald's wounds. He introduced Annabelle to Donald.

"I'm about to change his dressings. Would you care to assist me?"

She looked uncertain. He understood this was all new to her. "I'll explain everything as I work, so you'll comprehend what I'm doing."

She nodded. "I'll certainly do my best." Her smile eased away her worry lines.

"Good. I admire determination." A vision of Teena's firm expression as she informed him he would help her momentarily blurred his concentration.

He scrubbed his hands, dried them and set out his supplies, all the time explaining what he was doing and why. He removed the soiled dressing on the abdominal wound and sighed his relief when he saw it looked clean. "No redness or pus or swelling. All good signs." He glanced over his shoulder at Annabelle. She pressed her lips together. She had grown very pale. "Are you okay?"

She swallowed hard and nodded.

He redressed the wound and checked the foot. It, too, looked healthy. This time when he glanced at Annabelle her color was good. He rose and squeezed her shoulder. "You're doing great."

She followed him outdoors. "I must go home now. What time would you like me tomorrow?"

His patients arrived from dawn to dusk but he could hardly ask her to appear at the unearthly hour of four in the morning. "I'll have to start regular hours. Come about eight."

With a little wave and a gentle smile, she marched away, swinging her parasol over her shoulder.

Jacob watched until she rounded the corner, out of sight. He turned to clean up the soiled dressings and came face-to-face with Margie scowling at him something fierce.

"I suppose you think that's what a woman should be like."

"I have no idea what you mean."

"Dressed all fancy, like dirt don't stick to her. Hiding her true feelings 'neath a false smile."

"Margie, I need a nurse to help me. She's offered."

"She ain't the first one, if I recall."

He sidled around her. As far as he was concerned, this conversation wasn't taking place.

"You need to look past the outside of a person and see what's inside. Not all of us fit into some pretty little mold. Nor do we want to." She huffed away, muttering about men and how she would never understand them.

Jacob stared after her. Why was she so upset? He shrugged and returned to his task. Who could understand a woman like her? He caught the murmur of voices—recognized Margie's strident tones and then Teena's soft reply.

If only Teena didn't practice shaman medicine based on superstition and ignorance.

But she did.

And that kind of care had cost his brother his life. He dared not allow any of it into his clinic.

Chapter Five

"You should march over there and tell him to open his eyes," Margie said to Teena. "Pshaw. Men can be so blind."

Why had Jacob invited someone else to learn from him when she had wanted it so badly? Teena pushed her hurt and disappointment into the dark corners of her mind. She'd prayed. She'd tried to have faith, as Mack had said on Sunday. But faith and doubt and disappointment warred within her. Maybe answers to prayer were reserved for the white man. Oh, yes, sometimes God granted her request, but perhaps only if it helped a white person.

She turned back to Margie, forcing a reluctant smile to her lips. "I can watch them and learn." It wasn't enough. She ached to ask why, be shown how to do it herself.

Margie tossed her hammer to the floor of the clinic. "I'm in no mood to hang about here. Let pretty little Annabelle finish the building. I'm leaving."

"Where are we going?"

"Anywhere but here." She stomped away, called over her shoulder. "No reason you should hang about, either."

Teena looked at the half-finished building. Dr. Jacob really needed it done. She lifted one shoulder and sighed. Little she could do on her own. It had been a few days since she'd checked the trail for anyone injured or sick. Grabbing up her pack, she slipped away. But as she walked, her thoughts remained stubbornly at the clinic, wishing for a way to learn the white man's methods so she could help her people.

Margie showed up again the next morning.

"I wondered if you would come back," Teena said.

"I never hold a grudge. 'Sides, the doctor needs us." She handed Teena a length of wood. "Let's get the inside walls done."

People—mostly men—lined up on the sidewalk.

One by one, Dr. Jacob called them forward into his tent. He touched each wrist, as Teena had seen him do before, with his long, steady fingers. Sometimes he put that thing in his ears and pressed the other end to the man's chest. But not always. Why not? How did he know when to use it and when not to? Often, he stuck a little stick of glass in the person's mouth and told them to hold it under their tongue. She'd never heard of giving powders or teas this way. It was so strange. If only he would allow her to watch and ask questions.

Annabelle pranced to Dr. Jacob's side. "I'm here to help."

A sigh rippled down the line of men.

Margie groaned. "I 'spect his business will pick up something fierce."

Teena giggled.

Annabelle hovered at Dr. Jacob's side. Although she didn't ask questions, the doctor explained everything he did.

Teena pressed close to the opening in the wall that would become a window, and eagerly listened as he talked.

The sliver of glass was called a thermometer. "It tells me the temperature of a person's body." He showed it to Annabelle, who seemed unable to see it without pressing close to the doctor. "If it is higher than this mark, it indicates an infection."

Teena strained to see what he meant, but it was too far and the glass too small. She shaped the word in her mouth. *Infection.* He'd used that word before…the first day she'd seen him, when he told her not to use her superstitious ways anymore. But she didn't know what it was or how he cured it.

Margie clattered about with pieces of lumber. "Person can't be expected to do everything theirself."

Teena reluctantly left her post and went to help Margie, but was soon drawn back to watch and listen. The line of waiting men had grown longer.

Teena glanced at the closest men. None of them looked at all sick, to her way of thinking. Yet, one by one they eagerly dropped gold dust into the tin Dr. Jacob kept close. Did he not realize they had come to see Annabelle? Not that she cared, so long as she could listen to what he said.

A pair of men whom she'd seen around the store stood on the edge of the sidewalk waiting to see the doctor. Something about them edged along Teena's nerves like a sharp knife, and it was more than that they were dirty and unshaven. It was the way their eyes darted about, snooping through Dr. Jacob's belongings, spying on everyone's conversation.

Dr. Jacob called them forward. "What's ailing you two?"

The taller, thinner one coughed. "Gots me some lung problems."

Dr. Jacob pressed his instrument to the man's chest. "Sounds clear to me."

"Hurts awful when I cough." He gave a half-convincing demonstration, all the while his eyes examining, his ears twitching. "Heard Mack Tanner was telling youse about his gold treasure."

"Uh-huh." Jacob was not interested.

"Buried it up on the trail, I hear."

"If you say so. Try to keep dry and your cough will go away." He signaled the second man…stockier, and with narrow eyes that revealed no hint of kindness.

Teena shuddered. He was the sort of man who would shoot an Indian just for the joy of seeing him bleed.

"What can I do for you?" Jacob asked.

"It's me teeth." He opened his mouth and pointed inside.

Jacob pressed the man's tongue down with a silver knife. The blade was blunt, unlikely to hurt even the most tender flesh. "You have a rotten molar. I could pull it for you."

"How much?"

Jacob named a price.

The man considered it.

Teena's attention was not on the man Jacob examined. The first man had edged away. He lifted the tent flap and peered in—backed away and visually inspected several bundles as he inched toward the clinic. She eased into the shadows.

Margie, however, stomped forward and met the man in the open doorway. "Somethin' I can help you with?"

The man grinned, though his eyes continued to dart around the room. "Just curious. Guess this here is where the doc is going to set up shop." He lounged against the doorjamb as if Margie had invited him for tea. "Betcha hear lots, hanging about like this."

Margie didn't budge. "Don't have a mind to stick my nose in other people's business."

"Just saying. Like maybe you know where old Tanner has buried his gold."

"And I guess you think I'd tell you so's you could go dig it up."

The man put on a hurt expression. "Just wondering how much of the story is true, is all."

"Well, best you go ask Mack. Reckon he'll shore 'nough tell you."

"No need to be all prickly." He stepped closer. "Say, why don't you and me have us some fun?"

Teena could have warned the man he might not like Margie's idea of fun, but she didn't have a mind to spare him any grief.

Margie picked up a length of lumber, slammed it against the wall so close to the man that he likely thought he'd been bitten.

He jumped back and said a nasty word. "What's wrong with you?"

"Nothing a good laugh doesn't cure." And she laughed heartily.

Teena pressed her fingers to her mouth and enjoyed silent amusement.

The man huffed away, returned to his friend and waited while Dr. Jacob pulled the tooth and pressed a white bit of cloth into the man's mouth. Teena wished he would let her offer him a bit of mare's tail to stop the bleeding.

Men came all day long. Several times, Dr. Jacob had to make them wait while he boiled his tools and pulled more supplies from his bag.

"Annabelle, take this notebook and go down the line. Get everyone's name and ask them what's wrong. That way I can see to the most urgent cases first."

Margie whooped as Annabelle did as he'd suggested. "Look at the men. They crowd around her like metal shavings to a magnet. I betcha half of them would be cured if she just promised she'd accompany them to dinner. Pshaw. Men are such fickle creatures. Likely half them have wives back home." She made another rude noise. "Conveniently forgotten." She mumbled something about Lucy marrying one of those creatures, her words more than half-drowned by a great clattering of boards.

"Poor Dr. Jacob is looking wore out. If only he would let me help him."

"Why? He's got hisself pretty little Annabelle." Margie pranced across the floor, waving her hand in what she likely thought was a pretty gesture. On her it looked so out of place that Teena giggled.

But she would never be any more like Annabelle than Margie could be. A great heaviness settled about her shoulders like the feeling she had when her clan left the summer fishing camps and returned to the clan house for the winter. She missed the sun and would not see it again in blazing strength until spring. Or perhaps it was more like when her mother had died with the pox, and she knew she would never see her mother again. Never sit at her side listening to stories of the family, or getting instruction about the healing plants. This heaviness carried the weight of both. A missing of something elemental and internal.

She pushed to her feet. "The day is almost gone. I am going to cook a meal for my father." It was earlier than she usually went home to the village, but perhaps in her own quarters, among her own people, her mood would lighten.

* * *

Her father sat in the sunshine as she slipped from the shadows of the trail leading to the village. He glanced up as she approached. "You have come home."

"I will always come home."

"I hope so. But I fear you will leave us for the white man's world."

"Why would I do that?" Someone had brought them a basket of fish. She built a cooking fire outdoors. Soon enough the weather would cool and they would be cooking inside. She thought of the windows Dr. Jacob planned to put in his clinic. They would do little good during the dark hours of the Alaskan winter, and in the summer he would endure almost constant light and yet, the idea of being able to see out from indoors appealed to her. What kind of Tlingit was she, to be approving a white man's way? "I will cook you supper. Have you seen Jimmy since morning?"

"He is busy collecting gold."

"He works hard for it."

"He should be fishing. What will we eat this winter? Must we depend on others to feed us?" He waved toward the fish with disgust. "I will join the others tomorrow at the fishing camp."

"No, Father. You aren't well enough." He could barely walk across the yard unassisted. She feared anything strenuous would kill him. But perhaps it was time for her to give up her dream and join the rest of her clan. The heaviness settled over her again. She was not ready to abandon her quest. *God, if You listen to a Tlingit, give me a way to learn about healing. I must know if You will answer my prayer by two Sundays from now—ten days away.* If she didn't see any progress by then, she must abandon the idea and join the others in gathering food.

She jolted as an idea brushed her mind. Perhaps God would send another doctor who would welcome Teena's help. Maybe Dr. Jacob wasn't the answer to her prayer at all.

An ache weaved up her backbone and made her hurt all over. She didn't want to learn from another. She wanted it to be Jacob.

"What is it, Daughter?" her father asked.

Had she moaned aloud or had her father simply felt her pain. "I am fine." She brushed away her feelings with a silent prayer. *God, please let Jacob be the one to teach me.*

As soon as she finished the thought she wished she could recall it. She had no right for such a selfish request. No wonder God didn't hear her prayers.

Despite such condemning knowledge and the accompanying shame, she hurried toward the clinic the next morning, fully expecting Annabelle would, for some reason, fail to show up and Dr. Jacob, pressed by so many sick people, would ask her to help.

He stood over the stove, watching a tray of instruments simmering on the fire.

She sidled up to him. "You are very busy."

He scrubbed at his chin. "My workload has tripled in the last few days."

She stifled a giggle. "The men appreciate looking at Annabelle."

"You think that's what it is?"

She ducked her head, amazed at how blind he could be. In so many ways. "I could do that for you." She indicated the instruments. "I listen and know what you need."

His hands grew still. He stared at the pan on the stove and drew in air like he wanted to suck in the wind. Then he looked at her.

She widened her eyes at the darkness in his face.

"Teena, I understand how much you want to help. How you want to learn our methods. But I cannot, in good conscience, subject my patients to native healing practices. They trust me to provide the latest scientific advances." He shook his head. "It's just not possible."

She tucked her pride about her and headed to the clinic to help Margie, but she glanced out the window so often, Margie tossed a board to the floor in exasperation. "You gonna help, or moon around after a man who sees you as less than him?"

"He doesn't... I'm not... Annabelle hasn't come yet."

"She'll show up in her sweet time. No way she's going to miss all this attention." Margie nodded toward the long line of men. "Seems everyone within hiking distance has an ailment." She snorted. "And if you believe that... Here, grab this board and hold it for me."

Teena did so. As she helped, a murmur rippled through the waiting men.

"Annabelle has arrived," Margie said.

Teena didn't need Margie to inform her, and she pretended a great interest in the building project to hide her disappointment. But she couldn't stay away from the window. Dr. Jacob explained something to Annabelle and gave her a smile full of gentleness.

Teena jerked back from her post. "I'll find Burns to help you. I'm leaving."

"Where you goin'?"

"Fishing. My father needs food."

"Well, fine." Margie was upset, but it couldn't be helped. Teena had to get away.

She wandered through the press of people, ignoring comments about her being a Tlingit, until she found Burns and persuaded him to help Margie, reminding him of his promise to Dr. Jacob.

She joined her friends and family at the fishing camp and for two days worked hard. It felt good to be helping, doing her share and especially being appreciated. No one here gave her sideways looks nor made rude comments. Yet it was a strangely empty feeling. What was Dr. Jacob doing while she fished? Did he even notice she was absent?

She would have missed attending church the next day, but her people didn't work on Sunday. They attended church. She could hardly avoid it, especially when Jimmy and Father intended to go and Jimmy needed her help to get Father there.

* * *

Jacob wondered if Teena would be at church this morning. Just as he wished he knew why she'd disappeared. He felt her absence in a way that didn't make sense. He had never wanted her hanging around the clinic. But when he observed her listening as he explained procedures to Annabelle, he'd purposely raised his voice. He'd foolishly thought she'd stay and learn vicariously. It soothed his conscience to throw her such crumbs.

As he approached the church building, Annabelle fell in at his side. "May I join you?" she asked.

"Of course." It would be rude not to offer his arm, but he hoped she didn't take it for anything more than good manners.

He led her to a pew and ushered her in, waited for her to settle her skirts about her before he sat down. Only then did he allow himself to glance about. His heart felt lighter when he saw Teena with her brother and an old man. Was it her father? If Teena came back to work he'd ask her.

He turned back, smiling as he joined in singing several hymns, then concentrated on Mack's message.

"That was a lovely service, wasn't it?" Annabelle asked, as people began to leave. "It's so refreshing to be in a gold-mining town with some Christian principles."

Jacob had been about to make a dash for the door and hesitated. Good manners dictated he respond to the woman, though he spent almost every waking hour with her, and had not felt a flicker of curiosity regarding her past or her future. "You've been in other gold-rush towns?"

She batted her eyes and offered a coy smile. "One or two."

He nodded, his attention drifting to the people exiting at the back. If Teena had a mind to avoid him she would be gone before he could reach her.

"I had my reasons," Annabelle added, leaving her words open-ended like a question, an invitation to ask more.

"I must leave at once." He pushed into the crowded aisle and edged his way to the back. But Teena and her family had already ducked outside. He finally made it out and stood looking over the milling crowd. Where had she gone? Then he saw the trio shuffling toward the trail leading to the Indian village and he tried to break through the press of people around him, wanting to speak to her, ask her to come back, demand to know why she had stopped coming.

He ground to a halt. Why was his heart pushing him one way while his mind pushed another? Wasn't this for the best?

Let her go.

But he couldn't. The clinic needed to be finished and Margie and Burns together made little progress. In fact, he wondered if they were purposely taking their time, or were they simply unmotivated? He helped when he could, but patients kept them busy most of the day. Wanting Teena back was about getting the building ready for use, he assured himself, and resumed his push toward Teena.

Before he reached her, Burns stopped her and they spoke together. He laughed and then stepped away, waving as the trio continued onward. Spying Jacob, Burns hurried to him. "Teena said she would come back tomorrow. Isn't that great?"

"If it gets the clinic finished, it is." He had no more reason to chase after her, and he joined Burns heading toward the clinic.

And he purposefully stuffed aside his unreasonable, unacceptable disappointment.

But tomorrow she would return. His feet felt lighter than usual.

He was up with the dawn next morning. Donald was feeling better and wanting to eat. Jacob decided he was well enough to do so and fried eggs for the man. Burns rolled out of bed a few minutes later, called to life by the smell of food. He sat facing the trail from the Indian village. "I wonder when she'll get here."

Jacob sat at the boy's side as they ate, hoping his own impatience wasn't so obvious.

Already men were congregating on the plank walk, waiting to be seen. He glanced down the row and saw none who appeared to need immediate attention. In fact, none seemed even remotely interested in him. He knew they would wait patiently until Annabelle came. He sighed. This was not how he imagined it would be to have help.

Teena stepped into sight, her gait smooth and graceful as a breath of wind. Just seeing her filled him with peace.

Burns jumped up, the pup at his side, and raced to meet her.

Jacob couldn't hear what Burns said but saw the flash of amusement on Teena's face and caught her tinkling laughter. He was glad the pair were friends, even if it made him feel old and alone.

"That was good, Doc," Donald said, handing over the empty plate. "I feel I ought to do something to help." He struggled weakly, trying to gain his feet.

Jacob turned his attention to his job, his duties and his patient. "You're not up to a full day's work yet. But soon."

Donald settled back with relief. "I think I'll just sit in the sunshine for a while, if you don't mind."

Jacob didn't mind at all, and quickly cleaned up the breakfast dishes, preparing to begin seeing the patients. He sighed wearily. He didn't wish ill on anyone, but he would gladly treat a real sick person rather than deal with all these lookee-sees come to peer at Miss Annabelle. Perhaps he could dispense with a good number of them before she showed up.

Margie strode into sight, stopping to lean back on her heels and give the new building a pleased look. "Ought to finish up enough today that you can move in by evening."

There was one piece of good news.

"We got finishing to do outside, but if you don't

mind us hammering, we can do it while you take care of people inside."

He didn't care what they did and said so, then turned his attention to those waiting on the sidewalk. As he spoke to man after man with minor ailments, he could hear Teena and Margie talking as they built partitions in the clinic.

According to his plans, there would be four main areas—the examining area then a ward for the seriously ill. Two beds would fit in comfortably, more, if he crowded them, though he hoped he would have no cause for such. The next room would provide an area for surgeries and the fourth would serve as living quarters and a place to sterilize equipment.

He was about halfway through the lineup when Mack showed up. "Jacob, we need you. There's been an accident down by the water."

So grateful to be called away it was shameful, he scooped up his doctor's bag and followed Mack at a trot. He pushed through the crowd and saw a man prostrate in a pool of blood. "What happened?"

"He jumped off this stack and fell on that bottle. When we rolled him over he was spurting blood. It's slowed some now."

Jacob fell to his knees beside the inert man. He didn't like the sound of spurting blood and ripped the man's shirt from him to discover a slash on the underside of his arm. It took but a moment to assess and decide no artery had been cut. He feared the man had passed out, on his way to death, but he had only knocked his head in his fall. He moaned as Jacob examined him, already regaining consciousness. "I need him carried to the clinic." Four men grabbed the injured person and hurried across the beach to deposit him in Jacob's outside examining room. What he wouldn't give for a little privacy and better facilities. He sewed up the man's cut and asked Annabelle to clean up the area.

She filled a basin with water and daintily dabbed at the dried blood.

Jacob wanted to tell her to give it a little more effort, but saw the rapt look on the man's face. A glance at the waiting men revealed the same expression. He turned away with a sigh. Let them enjoy it while they could. There'd be no pretty doctor's assistant up the trail and into the Klondike.

He was about to call the man next in line when Mack called from the beach. "Jacob, there's another injured man. He's bad hurt. Hurry."

Jacob followed him at a run. Boxes and crates were scattered as if tossed aside in a hurry. He saw the man and understood the stack of goods had fallen on him. He tried to guess how many pounds had struck the man, but it was impossible.

"It's my legs." The man's voice was harsh with pain, but at least he was conscious.

Both legs were broken and likely a few ribs. One leg had a bad gash that would require stitches. The leg would need traction to keep it in alignment. Whether the clinic was finished or not, he was about to admit his first patient. He gave the man a good dose of laudanum and instructed the men on transferring him to the stretcher. He sent two ahead. "Tell Margie we need to set up a bed." He told them where to find it.

Annabelle stood ready to assist as they approached, but she took one look at the deep cut on the man's leg and turned away. He didn't have time to deal with her, but she managed to sit down without fainting. He could use her help, but not if she was about to pass out. "I think I can manage without you," he said.

"Then I've got something to do at home." She forced herself to her feet and scurried away.

Margie rushed about, getting the bed in place as he shepherded the stretcher bearers inside. She glanced at the leg and shook her head. "Bad break there."

Teena hovered, eager to observe. At this moment, he wished Annabelle was half as keen. Instead, he called Mack and a couple of other men. "I'll need assistance here." He had every intention of saving the leg and seeing the man walk again. The man had mercifully passed out, but before he proceeded he needed one piece of information. "Anyone know this man's name?"

"Thad Sanders," one of the men said.

It was good to know the name of the man who would require his attention for the next few hours. He only hoped he could save the man's leg.

Chapter Six

Supplies needed to be transferred to the shelves in the clinic, and Teena gladly took on the task. It allowed her an opportunity to secretly observe Jacob and listen to his instructions as he worked over Thad Sanders. Again, that mask with someone dripping liquid to it. Anesthesia. As she watched Jacob pull the bone into place and attach a series of pulleys and weights, she silently praised the white man for making it possible for the injured to be fixed without severe pain. She'd seen the doctor sew wounds together before, but was still fascinated by the quickness of his fingers.

An hour later, Jacob finally straightened and stretched his back and neck.

She could rub his muscles with a mixture to ease his stiffness if he would let her. She smiled secretly. Fish would fly before that happened.

"He will need to be watched carefully." Jacob looked about. "Where's Burns?"

Teena slid out of sight. She didn't want to be the one to tell him the boy had gone fishing. Jacob didn't seem to view the pursuit very highly.

Margie made some sort of rumbling answer that said nothing. "I can stay with him."

"He must keep still."

Margie snorted. "He don't look like much. I think I can manage."

Teena covered a snicker. Margie could handle most men, if she had such a mind.

Jacob nodded. "Get yourself a stool. You might be here awhile."

Margie hurried outside and returned with one. She perched at Thad's bedside with a look of determination that made Teena want to warn the sleeping man not to challenge her.

Jacob rubbed his neck and sighed. "Burns seems to be missing whenever I need him," he mumbled as he returned to the dwindling line of men.

Teena slipped to Margie's side. "Is there anything I can do?"

Margie patted her arm. "See if you can get that door into place and the sawdust cleaned up."

Teena kept busy until long past the time she should have returned to the village to care for her father. It wasn't that she had so much to do. Nor even that she couldn't tear herself away from watching Jacob patiently deal with each person who came to him. No. It was a deep awareness that Burns should have returned.

Her restlessness grew until it could not be denied. She didn't say a word to anyone as she slipped away to find him. He had gone fishing, and of course could have changed his mind or sought another pursuit, but her heart called her toward the river. As she approached it she called, "Burns," at first softly and then louder. "Burns, can you hear me?"

She followed the water course several hundred yards, pausing to ask people if they'd seen him. No one else seemed concerned at his long absence, yet the strange sensation that he needed her would not leave and she hurried on, calling his name over and over.

She rounded a corner, sheltered by thick bush, and called again. "Burns."

A dog barked. Nothing unusual about that. There were a hundred dogs or more in and around town, any number of them barking at any given time, but she heard a familiar note in the bark, felt something pulling her onward. She saw Yukon standing on the riverbank, barking at the water. Silly dog. But where Yukon was, Burns would be close by. "Burns." She joined the pup and looked toward the river. And gave a cry of horror.

Burns. Facedown on the bank. She squinted at his back. Was he breathing? It didn't appear so, and she scrambled down to his side. Quickly, deftly, she felt his body—but could feel nothing amiss and cautiously turned him over. His lips were blue. His chest not rising and falling. She grabbed his arms and pumped them up and down, over his head, back to his side. "Breathe, Burns. Please breathe." But nothing.

Oh God, if ever I need You to hear me, it is now. Please make him breathe. Please.

She pushed on his chest. It was rigid. She must breathe for him and she pressed her mouth over his and blew air into his lungs. She did it again and again. Suddenly, he threw out a lungful of water and gasped in air on his own.

Thank You, God. Thank You for hearing me and answering my prayer.

Burns coughed. His breath rattled in and out. He made no effort to rise.

"Help," she called.

A man looked over the bank, saw her. "Ain't helping no Injun." He backed away.

"Help," she called again. "It's the doctor's friend. He's hurt."

A half-dozen men scrambled to her side.

"Take him to the doctor." She trotted at their side as two men carried the boy.

Two men ran ahead and warned Jacob. He rushed down the street to meet them. "Burns, are you okay?"

"I'm a little weak," he murmured, his voice a thread.

"What happened?" he demanded of the men.

"Don't know," one said. "We just offered to carry him here."

Jacob saw Teena then and faced her. "Did you find him?"

She nodded and her voice quivered slightly as she told him how he'd been facedown and not breathing.

Jacob scrubbed at his forehead, weariness drawing deep lines on his face. "He must have fallen in the river. He told me he can't swim." Without another word to her he ran after the men bearing Burns and directed them into the clinic.

Teena followed. Dr. Jacob wouldn't welcome her in his clinic, but she would not leave Burns until she knew for certain he was going to be okay.

A second bed had been hastily set up by Thad's, where Margie held her post, her attention barely flickering from the still-unconscious man. Teena understood how Margie felt—she'd fight to make sure this man recovered.

She was prepared to do the same for Burns, and stood in the shadows watching as Dr. Jacob examined him. Burns looked so young and vulnerable on the bed. Teena ached to be closer. To smooth his brow and comfort him. She didn't move, however, fearing Dr. Jacob would demand she leave if he noticed her.

"I think you'll live," he said after he'd checked Burns. "If you don't get pneumonia. I want you to stay in bed until I say otherwise. Can you tell me what happened?"

"Teena saved my life. Where is she?"

Teena stepped forward. "I'm here."

Burns reached for her hand. "You saved my life." He turned to Jacob.

Burns closed his eyes. His grasp on Teena's hand loosened. He was exhausted.

"Rest is the best thing for you." She slipped outside.

She would not give Dr. Jacob a chance to tell her to leave.

Margie's robust voice followed her. "Doc, I hate to be the one to say it, but you are a bullheaded, blind fool."

Teena didn't bother listening for Jacob's reply, but she grinned as she headed for her village. It was nice to have Margie defend her.

What did it matter what Jacob thought? At least Burns was okay. That's all that mattered.

Except it wasn't enough to cleanse her of the ever-widening ache in her heart.

The next morning she hurried back to the clinic, anxious to see how Burns fared during the night. He sat propped up on pillows, nursing a cup of tea. A portable screen hid a portion of Thad's bed. Dr. Jacob was behind it, tending to the man.

Teena slipped by, hoping to be unnoticed. "How are you?" she whispered.

Burns coughed. "Feeling better."

Thad moaned, "Doc, it hurts something awful."

"I'll give you something for the pain."

Teena knew he would pour a spoonful of liquid from the brown bottle. What was this special medicine? How was it made? If only she could ask him her burning questions.

Burns coughed again, his lungs sounding spongy and hot.

Teena knew a mixture of plants that would aid in healing his lungs. The leaves from marsh marigold would be especially helpful. But no doubt Dr. Jacob had a more powerful medicine.

"Teena?" Dr. Jacob's voice came from behind the cloth covered screen.

Oh, no. He was going to chase her out. Forbid her to even visit Burns.

"Would you get Annabelle for me, please?"

"Okay." She trotted silently from the room. The usual line of men waited on the sidewalk, willing to pay their precious gold to visit the doctor, but mostly eager to pay to see Miss Annabelle up close. She bit back the urge to tell them to leave the good doctor alone. He had real work to do. A quick glance revealed Annabelle had not yet arrived, and she slipped inside to inform Dr. Jacob. A tiny, secret part of her hoped he would ask her out of desperation.

Instead, he said, "Is Margie there?"

"She's outside somewhere."

"Ask her to come."

Slowly, she left the room and located Margie sitting against the far wall of the building, holding a cup of tea. "You look tired."

"I stayed with Thad until Dr. Jacob chased me away. He said I should get sleep, but I didn't want to leave Thad. He's in some misery. He gripped my hand all night. Seemed to feel better if I was there talking to him. Is Jacob with him now?"

"He is, and wants you."

Margie lumbered to her feet, jogged around the corner and out of sight.

Teena glanced about. The plan had been to finish siding the clinic, but she wondered if the resulting noise would disturb the patients. Instead, she'd clean up the littered building material and half-unpacked crates.

A frantic man shoved his way through the waiting crowd. "I need a doctor. A doctor. Where is he?" He rushed toward the clinic hollering, "Doctor?"

Jacob stepped to the doorway. "What seems to be the problem?"

"My wife. She's having a baby but something's wrong. She needs you. Hurry."

Jacob glanced about. Annabelle sauntered into sight. "You're here. Good." He spoke to the anxious man. "I'll just leave some instructions for the patients, then I'll join you." He ducked back inside, Annabelle following at a leisurely pace.

Teena tried not to judge the woman. After all, she was what a white woman was expected to be. Dressed in wide skirts, her hair all fancied up. Teena glanced at her own simple gray skirt and blouse, over which she wore the usual woven shawl with red pattern. She dressed plain. She cared not what people thought of her. Most days. But she knew how to work, how to hurry, how to care for a hurting person.

Dr. Jacob's firm tones came from inside, instructing Annabelle as to what she should watch for, then he stepped from the building, his black leather bag swinging from one hand. He saw Teena and hesitated a moment.

If her eyes could speak he would surely see how

much she wanted to accompany him, but he only looked uncertain. "I'll be back as soon as I can."

She smiled, her heart round with happiness that he had given this promise to her.

Those waiting on the sidewalk saw he was leaving. They realized Miss Annabelle would be occupied indoors and slipped away.

Teena tried to think what to do. Should she go home and spend time with her father? Go to the fishing camp? But neither idea appealed. It had been a couple of days since she'd climbed the Chilkoot looking for injured people. There might be dozens needing help.

But her heart called her to stay. Quietly she stepped inside.

Margie hung over Thad's bed. "Listen to me, you big lug. You ain't gonna die. Not while I'm here."

Thad gave a weak chuckle. "Whatever you say, Margie." He sounded mellow, happy.

Margie laughed heartily. "Good thing you've a mind to listen to me." She saw Teena. "You tell him what happens to men who argue with Margie."

Teena smiled. "They soon learn not to."

Thad's grin was lopsided and uncertain as he looked up at Margie. "I'll be just fine, so long as you're here to take care of me."

Annabelle glared at Teena, all pretense of niceness gone. "You know the doctor forbids you to come in here."

Teena smiled gently. Dr. Jacob hadn't said those exact words, but she wasn't about to argue. Assured Burns rested quietly, she backed from the room and slipped away. She would cook her father a big pot of fish stew laced with lots of healing herbs.

Her father greeted her softly when she arrived home. "You spend too much time with the white men. You will soon be one of them."

"No, Father." Her mouth said the words but her heart didn't follow. Not that she wanted to be one of them, but she did want one in particular to see her with kind eyes. She stirred up the fire and added ingredients to the pot.

"You haven't forgotten you are promised to Tom Wolf."

"I haven't forgotten." Though the promise was made by her father, not by her. She had no feelings for the man. Could barely think what he looked like, although she had seen him enough times. The only face she could conjure up in her thoughts was…

Her thoughts needed taming, and she carefully closed the door to them.

She stirred more things into the pot and bent low to sniff the aroma. "Doesn't this smell delicious?"

"I don't have much appetite."

"You will not regain your strength if you don't eat."

"I'm an old man." He sounded so weary that Teena spun to confront him.

"It is not your time to die."

He studied her silently, his expression sorrowful. "Who says when it is time?"

She tore her gaze away, silenced her arguments and renewed her vow to learn the white man's ways of healings. *God, I know You answered when I asked for Burns to start breathing again, but I don't know if I can ask for my father. He's a Tlingit. But he is a good man. He needs to grow strong again. Is it possible for You to do something powerful for him? And for me? Dr. Jacob does not want to teach me his ways. But I must learn them.*

Her insides ached at how many had died because she knew not how to help them.

Please, God. Open Dr. Jacob's heart. Make him want to teach me.

She tidied the clearing as she visited with her father. But after a few minutes he grew tired. She let him rest until the stew was ready, then shook him gently. "Father, eat. It will give you strength."

He took the steaming bowl she offered and brought a spoonful to his mouth. She didn't leave his side until he ate most of the contents.

"Leave me now." His arm straight, he lifted one hand in a familiar gesture, reminding her of his former strength. "I am tired. I will sleep in the sun."

She offered the rest of the stew to the other members of the clan and they accepted gratefully. The strengthening herbs would benefit them, too. Sonda, the new mother, would surely have stronger milk so the little one would not be so weak. And old Auntie May would soon be wanting to go to the fishing camp.

Teena knew she only wanted to see these things. Her people were weak from a season of disease. White man's diseases.

She must learn how to heal those diseases.

"I am going back to Treasure Creek." She didn't care if no one heard her announcement. She was speaking to herself as much as anyone. She would not come back until Dr. Jacob agreed to teach her.

How she hoped to persuade him to do so, she couldn't say.

As she neared the clinic she saw Annabelle outside, seated on one of the stools, a circle of men around her.

Teena paused, then ducked up the side street so she could approach from the back and slip inside without Annabelle noticing.

A minute later, she stepped into the building and her nerves tensed. Burns was moaning and muttering. His tortured breathing rattled across the room. She ran to his side, touched his forehead. He was burning up.

Where was Margie? Thad slept peacefully. She must have gone to get some rest, but why wasn't Annabelle looking after Burns?

He gasped in air, fighting to fill his lungs, his eyes wide with alarm. He tried to speak, but it only made him cough.

"Don't talk. I will take care of you." She helped him sit so he could breathe easier. "I'm going to make you something to ease your lungs." She hesitated, afraid to leave him alone.

Margie stepped into the room. "Burns is in bad shape. I went looking for the doctor. He was seen heading up the pass with that man who called him to help his wife deliver a baby. I thought the woman was on the beach, but seems I was wrong."

"Stay with him. I'm going to make him tea that will fix him."

Margie came to Burns's side, her expression wreathed in doubt. "The doctor said—"

"I know, but I will not stand by and watch a man suffer when I know how to fix it." For this, she did not need white man medicine.

Margie nodded. "Don't guess you can make him any worse."

Teena slipped out and put a pot of water on the stove. As she waited for it to boil, she opened her bag and pulled out several leaf-wrapped packages.

Annabelle studied her a moment, then harrumphed and returned to her admirers. "Crazy Indian."

The men chuckled at her dismissive tone, but Teena paid them no mind. She had more important things to do.

She stirred the leaves and powder into the boiling water and let it steep a few minutes to draw out the goodness, then she added water to cool it and carried the pot and a cup into the clinic. She poured the mixture into the cup and held it to Burns's lips. "Drink."

It was all he could do to spare the energy from

breathing to swallow, but gulp by gulp, he emptied the cup.

She let him rest a moment, then insisted on him taking another cupful.

Great beads of perspiration appeared on his brow. "Good. It is working."

A second cup and a third disappeared down Burns's throat.

As she offered a fourth, he held up a hand in protest. "Enough."

"Not enough. You must drink until your cough is loose and your breathing easy." It usually took about five cupfuls with a Tlingit. She could never be certain a white man would respond the same way.

But by the end of the fifth cup, Burns had started to cough, bringing up gunk. "It will clear your lungs," she assured him. His breathing eased considerably.

He lay down, exhausted.

She washed his face, wiping off the sweat pouring from him. "This is all good. Very good."

Burns grinned. "I feel a lot better." He made to sit up and swayed. "Maybe not that good." He lay back down.

"I think you will rest a few days." She sat at his side, singing softly in Tlingit, the songs that brought comfort, and he fell asleep.

Margie sat at Thad's bedside. "Well, ain't that somethin'? Won't the doc be surprised?"

"Please don't tell him." He would be very angry. How

could she hope to persuade him to teach her if he knew she had gone against his wishes?

Margie shook her head. "I don't understand. Seems you'd want him to realize your ways have something to offer."

"I do. But not until he's ready."

Annabelle peeked in the doorway. "I see everything is fine. I'll just wait outside."

Margie rolled her eyes. "She doesn't even realize what happened. Burns could have died, for all the attention she gave him."

But it wasn't over with. Twice more Burns grew hot and his chest tightened. Twice more she forced him to drink the tea. By then the sky was dusky with the short night.

Still Dr. Jacob had not returned.

Teena went to the doorway and stared toward the trail. Where had he gone? Did he need help?

She stuffed back a giggle. One day he would see how he needed her help, but he did not yet realize it.

The next morning Jacob trudged down the trail, ignoring the climbers, not seeing the debris cluttering the edges, aware only of the ignorance of men who would drag a woman in the latter stages of her confinement up a mountain that conquered many a man, and expect her to survive. He'd stayed all night and done everything he could to help, but it hadn't been enough. The mother died as the baby was delivered. The babe cried and then was silent. In the end, he lost them both.

It was so unnecessary. If the woman had been in Seattle, she would still be alive, loving her sweet baby girl.

"I can't wait to get away from this place," he muttered, not caring if anyone thought him odd in talking to himself. Truth was, they had probably seen worse, even acted worse at times. These people were crazy with gold fever. Mack told him it was even more insane in the winter. He didn't want to think it could be.

Such ignorant behavior was inexcusable. He paused and stared at the sky. Why did God tolerate men's stupidity?

Or did He? Seems a person reaped what they sowed, and if a man sowed greed and recklessness, he reaped a harvest of pain and disappointment, as the man up the mountain had.

He reached the bottom of the trail and headed for the General Store to find Mack. He found him easily enough—surrounded by a dozen clamoring men. Jacob wondered how Mack could make out all the demands. He told the man missing part of a shipment to speak to Caleb Johnson.

"He's the harbormaster. He'll have information on the ship's cargo."

Someone else wanted to know where he could find a guide over the mountains, another asked if there was a list of men willing to pack a load across the pass. Still another complained about the mud—as if Mack had the power to cure the problem. A tough-looking pair, who appeared better suited to herding cows than climbing steep mountain trails, threatened to do something drastic if the supplies they'd ordered didn't arrive on the next boat.

"I have no control over when my orders come." Mack rubbed his brow and sighed, a sound so full of weariness, Jacob gave him a harder look and pushed his way to the front of the line.

"You're looking wore out. Can't you leave some of this stuff to others to handle?"

Mack leaned back against the counter. "I try. But it seems, as Mayor of Treasure Creek, I am expected to know all the answers and have solutions to all the problems."

"I regret I'm here to add to your load." He told about the deaths of the woman and child.

"Does he need help getting them off the mountain?"

"I found Jimmy Crow and sent him. But they'll need a proper burial when they get here."

"Of course they will. I'll say a few words over them. Sure wish I could persuade Thomas Stone to take on the job of preacher. I'm not cut out for it, nor do I feel I am able to devote the time to it that I should."

Jacob clamped the man's shoulder. "You're doing a fine job, so far as I can see." But it was too much for any man. Goodness knew, life on its own in this raw, wild country was too much for him. "Put out a notice, both here and in Dawson City, for a doctor to take my place."

Mack grabbed Jacob's arm. "Don't let this get you down. I'd like to see you stay."

Jacob shuddered at the idea of spending any more time here than necessary to achieve his goal. He'd leave today if there was someone to take his place. "I have a practice waiting for me back in Seattle." His current responsibilities weighed on his shoulders. "And two patients in the clinic." He'd left instructions with Annabelle on what to watch for and what to do if Burns or Thad spiked fevers, but he wouldn't be at peace until he made sure they were okay.

Annabelle met him at the doorway. It was two hours until regular hours started, when she normally came.

He almost stumbled at the sight of her. "You're here early. Or did you spend the night?" He'd expected Margie would step in and make sure the patients were not left alone. Annabelle seemed a bit too frail to give up a night's sleep.

"Just doing my duty, making sure everything is taken care of in your absence. You look tired. Can I send to the restaurant for a meal for you?"

Her concern was touching. "I must check the patients first." Wearily, he looked at the line of waiting men. He suspected very few were truly ill. Hadn't they had enough gawking at Annabelle yet? He wished they would find another way of getting their chance to look. He was tired of this whole charade. Ignorance. Greed. Recklessness. He couldn't get back to Seattle fast enough for his peace of mind.

He stepped inside, Annabelle clinging to his side.

At a glance, he saw Burns rested quietly. Margie sat at Thad's side. "Have you been here all night?"

Thad answered. "She's making sure I get better."

"How are you?"

"Doc, I gotta confess I've felt better in my life. And I can't remember feeling worse. Not even once."

Jacob laughed. "You're feeling well enough to complain. That's a good sign. Let's have a look at your leg." The ribs would heal in their good time, but the leg stood a chance of infection, and the worst possible thing— gangrene. "So far so good," he said after checking the wound. "Too bad you have to lie still until it heals."

"I *will* walk again?"

"I don't make any promises, but if it heals I expect you'll be climbing mountains soon enough."

Thad sighed. "Don't know if my heart's in climbing mountains anymore."

Too bad it took a disaster to make the man change his mind.

He moved to Burns's side.

The boy opened his eyes and grinned.

Relief whooshed through Jacob. He'd grown unreasonably fond of the boy and feared his near-drowning would kill him. "How are you feeling?"

"Tons better than yesterday."

Annabelle sidled up to Jacob. "The boy was hot yesterday, but I remembered what you said to do, and here he is. As good as new."

Jacob wondered at Margie's snort, but signaled them all to be quiet as he listened to Burns's lungs. He sighed his satisfaction. The boy would recover. It almost made up for losing the woman and child during the night.

"Jacob—" Burns began but Annabelle cut him off.

"Jacob, you need to eat and rest. Come along. I'll take care of you."

Almost past the point of thinking, Jacob allowed her to gently lead him away.

"Jacob," Burns called. "I gotta talk to you."

"I'll be back in a bit." Suddenly, food and a rest sounded essential. He followed Annabelle outside and sat while she sent for a meal and prepared to make tea.

Margie stomped out the door. "Doc, you better come here."

He bolted to his feet. "Thad?" So many things could go wrong, and so quickly.

"Come see for yourself." She headed back inside, taking it for granted he'd follow, and he did.

Annabelle grabbed his arm. "I'm sure it can wait until you've eaten."

"Some things can't wait." He rushed after Margie, fearing all sorts of disasters.

Inside the clinic, Margie, her arms crossed, glared at him from the foot of Thad's bed. Burns sat on the edge of his bed, a dark frown on his face. Even Thad seemed unhappy.

He skidded to a halt. "What's wrong?"

"I just about died yesterday," Burns said, his voice ringing with accusation.

"I'm sorry I wasn't here." His trek up the mountain

had been in vain. "But Annabelle took care of you." It was something to be grateful for.

"No, Annabelle did not."

"Then what…?"

"Teena did."

The skin on the back of his neck tingled. "You didn't let her give you something, did you? I can't imagine the harm it could do you."

"Doc, you need to listen." Margie practically snarled. "She saved his life."

"Did she give him something?"

Annabelle had followed. "I tried to stop her but…" She shrugged, indicating how helpless she was before a determined Teena.

Margie didn't so much as flick a glance at Annabelle, her gaze drilling Jacob. "Whatever it was, it fixed him. Before she gave it, he could barely breathe and he was burning up with fever."

"I thought I made it clear she was not to practice her malarkey here."

Margie took a step toward him, her expression as threatening as her stance, and he backed away.

Thad chuckled. "Think you best listen to her, Doc."

Margie didn't wait for him to decide if he'd listen or not. She faced him, her eyes narrowed. "Doc, I don't know how many times I told you to stop being so short-sighted."

He couldn't remember her ever telling him, but decided he wouldn't say so. Not that she gave him a chance to protest as she roared on.

"I said you need to look beyond what you see with your eyes. Up here in the North, we don't measure each other by fine clothes." She snorted. "Nor by the color of a person's skin. You don't need to be here long to realize we can learn from everyone. Either good or bad." She leaned closer. "I figure you've been here long enough to know that. Yet you're still blind when it comes to Teena." Her face was now inches from his.

He swallowed hard. "I have no idea what you mean."

Margie sniffed. "Then you aren't the intelligent man you make out to be."

"If you were a man, I might take offense at that." He kept the rancor from his voice.

"I mean no offense, but it's time you opened your eyes."

"My eyes *are* open." He tried to stare her down.

"I wonder. If they are, you'll take a good look at your friend Burns and bear in mind he almost died. I figure he would of, if it depended on Annabelle."

Behind him, Annabelle made a strangled sound of protest. "I did exactly what the doctor said."

Margie shifted from glaring at Jacob to scowling at Annabelle. Jacob guessed being indoors was the only thing that kept her from spitting. "Think you might want to wait outside while I talk to the doc."

He didn't turn to see if Annabelle stayed or left, but he pushed past Margie's stubborn figure. Time to uncover the truth for himself. "Burns, let's hear what happened."

"I couldn't breathe," he began. "She made a bitter tea and made me drink it. Lots of it. And now look at me. I'm ready to get up."

"Not yet." Jacob considered the situation. She'd given Burns something, but rather than kill him, it supposedly had made him better. Aaron had been treated by a native shaman and died. The reports he and Mother had received made it clear the shaman was responsible for his death. In fact, according to the information, the native healer had poisoned Aaron—perhaps inadvertently, but it didn't change the fact that Teena's methods were risky at best.

Margie cleared her throat to get his attention. "Doc, there was no mumbo jumbo. She didn't wave a fistful of feathers over him. Just made him drink the tea. Made it from leaves. I saw myself how it helped."

"She's speaking the truth," Thad said.

Jacob scrubbed at his neck. He was tired. So tired that none of this made sense. "I need to eat." He hurried outside. Annabelle held a covered plate.

"They sent bacon, eggs, fried potatoes and what looks like an apple dumpling." Her smile was sweet, though gently chiding.

Jacob didn't say anything beyond thanks. He consumed the large plateful of food and began to feel human again, but his brain was still in a knot. He pushed to his feet. "I'll be back shortly." He strode toward the woods surrounding the town, hoping for some peace and quiet so he could think.

He passed the church, saw the cemetery out back and turned toward it. He'd seen the crosses and markers plenty of times. The information they'd received said Aaron was buried there. He'd never had the stomach to look before, but now he entered the still graveyard and wandered up and down the rows, the sound of tumbling water in the background, until, finally, he found a marker with the name Aaron Calloway and the date of his death several months ago. His knees folded of their own accord and he sank to the ground in front of the crude wooden cross. He touched the roughness. As soon as he got back to Seattle he would order a proper marker. Why had Aaron died? Was God punishing the family for something they'd done or failed to do? It had caused his mother's sudden decline, as well, so Jacob could only assume the punishment was meant for him. *I've tried to live an honorable life. Always. Where have I failed?* He couldn't think of anything, though he didn't presume to think he was perfect by any means.

Had the shaman who treated Aaron been like Teena? Or was Teena different? A healer, in her primitive way?

He had to face the truth. She might be primitive by many standards, but she seemingly had saved Burns's life. He had no reason to believe otherwise.

But what was he to do with the information?

Judge not that ye be not judged. It was a verse from Scripture. But how did it apply?

Be fair.

He stared up at the bright sky. Was he unjustly blaming Teena for something she had nothing to do with? She had helped Burns. In fact, to his knowledge, everyone she had in some way doctored had recovered.

He knew he was wrong in holding her responsible for Aaron's death, but his pride put up a struggle.

Pride goeth before a fall. Hadn't his mother warned him of that many times? Likely, his pride was the reason for the bad things in his life. They were his punishment. He vowed he would conquer it. His mind made up, he pushed to his feet.

Teena had not been at the clinic. No doubt afraid of his anger when he found out she had treated Burns against his wishes. But he would find her and give her a chance to explain what she'd done.

He would not judge her ways until he knew more than anger at Aaron's unnecessary death.

He looked around. Should he go up the trail leading to the pass, or down the path toward the Indian village? Where was she?

Chapter Seven

He finally chose the path to the village and trod through the striped shadows until he broke into the blue-white sunlight of the site.

Teena stood waiting, her expression guarded, yet she met his eyes across the clearing without flinching.

The sun flooded her features as if she were lit from the inside. She was as beautiful as she was gentle. And equally stubborn and strong. She'd endured much unfairness, not only from him, but from others, yet she remained unfazed. At least outwardly. He couldn't help think the cruelness hurt her inwardly. A pain speared through him. He been as guilty as any by judging Teena, putting her in the same category as he had the shaman responsible for Aaron's death.

She turned and spoke to an old man behind her. The same shrunken man he'd seen her with at church. Then she called to Jacob. "Please, come and say hello to my father." With a graceful sweep of her arm she invited him to join her. She bowed before her father and spoke in her native tongue, then stepped back as she said, "Dr. Jacob Calloway."

The old man's skin was leathery from years out in the cold and heat. His cheeks were sunken, the skin pocked. Jacob suspected he'd survived smallpox. His illness had left him emaciated, yet his dark eyes snapped with intelligence as he studied Jacob.

Without speaking, Jacob waited under the man's inspection.

Then the man scowled and he spoke harshly to Teena.

"What did he say?" Jacob asked.

Teena's smile trembled at the edges, as if her father's words saddened her. "You do not want to know."

Her father dismissed Jacob with a flick of his hand. Jacob backed away. "Is he angry at me?"

"He's angry at me."

"You? What have you done?"

She ducked her head so he couldn't see her eyes. "He blames me that you are here."

"I'm sorry. I didn't know." He was struck with the irony of it—so many white men angry when a native crossed the threshold of one of the businesses in town, and now a native angry that a white man had stepped into his village. "I came to ask you—" He stopped. If he asked what she'd done it would sound condemning. He didn't mean to be. "It seems you saved Burns's life yesterday." He'd been unfair, refusing to admit what he saw in her. And even worse.

What he felt about her. "I want to thank you. I also failed to thank you for rescuing him from a near-drowning. I'm sorry for my neglect."

They had slowly been making their way back to the tree-shrouded trail and she paused, her head bent down. "I only did what I must do."

"What is that?"

"I must help the white man when he is sick or injured."

"Must?" It seemed a strange reason. "Why?"

She slowly lifted her head. Although the shadows made it hard to see her expression clearly, he guessed she wondered how much she wanted to tell him. "Why do you ask?"

He wasn't sure he understood his reasons. "I'm just curious. And I'm trying to understand a few things."

She nodded. "Then I will tell you my story. When I was only so big—" she held her hand at waist height "—the missionary came with news of God, the Great Creator. We knew about Him already, but feared His anger."

Justly so, Jacob thought. He, too, feared displeasing a righteous God.

"But Mr. McIntyre, the missionary man, told us God's son, Jesus, became a man and was punished for our sins, although He Himself did not sin, so we could be right with God."

Jacob nodded, wondering what this had to do with her reason for helping white men.

"We had heard the news before from Russian

missionaries, but this time we understood and believed."
Her expression softened. "We are grateful he brought
us good news."

"So you owe all white men?"

"I have not finished my story."

"Sorry. Go on."

"Mr. McIntyre had a daughter the same size as me.
Sarah was her name. Sarah and I were special friends.
We fit here." She touched her chest. "Heart friends. We
did much together. One day, we followed my brother,
Jimmy, up the trail, although we were forbidden to do
so. It was fun jumping from rock to rock." She hung
her head in such a way that Jacob wondered why such
innocent play made her sad. "I knew the dangers," she
whispered. "How the rocks could suddenly come alive,
but I was too busy playing." She paused, sucking in air.
"The rocks started to move without warning, and so fast
I couldn't move out of their way. I screamed, trying to
think which way to run. Sarah rushed over and pushed
me out of the way."

The silence had a deepness to it that crinkled the
edges of Jacob's thoughts. "You were both okay,
though?"

Teena shuddered. "The rock struck her legs. They
were never right. She couldn't walk. I said I would carry
her every place she wanted to go, but after a while her
mother and father left. They headed south, where they
hoped she could be helped." The words tore from her
throat in such a way that Jacob knew they hurt deeply.

He wanted to ease her pain but didn't know how. So

often, he felt helpless in the face of suffering. "Have you heard from them since?"

She shook her head.

"No letters?" Seems they would have written.

"I do not read." She faced him squarely, as if daring him to show shock, or worse—disgust—which she'd no doubt seen more than her share of.

"That is why you help others?"

She nodded. "To repay what Sarah did for me. And because I know native healing ways." She watched him, waiting for his reaction.

"What do you use?"

"Plants. Healing plants."

He couldn't believe it was that simple.

"Different plants, different parts of them help different things."

"How do you know what plants work for what?"

"My mother and grandmother taught me. They learned from their mother and grandmother."

He indicated they should continue walking toward Treasure Creek, and as they walked he tried to assess the information she had shared. "No dancing and waving feathers?"

She chuckled. "Not our clan."

He heard a hesitation in her voice. "There's more?"

"I pray." She stopped walking and faced him, and in the thin, barred light, he caught a glimpse of something hungry and uncertain and again felt a strange urge to comfort her. Again, he did not know how.

"But I do not know if God grants the requests of a Tlingit."

Her agonized uncertainty slashed through him. "God is no respecter of persons."

"That is in the Holy Word, isn't it? Mr. McIntyre used to say it."

"God looks on the heart."

She pressed her palm to her chest, as if protecting her heart. Then she stood straight and tall, her hands at her side. "My heart belongs to God."

He pressed his hand to his chest as she had done. "Mine, too."

They studied each other openly, frankly, for the first time. A sense of something he could only explain as unity wrapped about them, though he could not say if she felt the same. Only that her eyes held his, dark and bottomless, opening to him with trust. He vowed he would treat her fairly from here on. No more judging her with the same anger he judged the shaman who killed Aaron. "Do all the people you help live?" It was a foolish question. She could no more save everyone than he could, but he hoped her words would enable him to make sense of the needless suffering and deaths he saw.

"Not all. Isn't a man's days in the Creator's hands, to give or take away according to His good plan?" She sighed deeply. "Besides, some seek help too late. Or don't take care of themselves."

"God's good plan, you say? So you believe everything is for our good?" He knew he should believe it as a Christian. Didn't the Scripture say, "All things work together for good to them that love God"? But did he love God enough? He could never be certain he did.

"I cannot answer such a big question. It is beyond me. One thing I know is that God is big, immense." She waved her arm in an all-encompassing sweep. "He made the world and everything in it." She plucked a leaf from a tree and examined it. "And yet He took the time to create a pattern on each leaf." She showed him. And he bent his head close to hers, aware of a not unpleasant musky scent—elemental and comforting, like the hint of yeasty baking, Christmas pines and contentment.

She lifted her head. Their gazes collided, hers full of mystery and belief. As their look went on, silently examining this new tenuous acceptance between them, something shifted inside him, as though a priceless gift had been placed in his hands. He both feared the responsibility and anticipated the enjoyment and reward of opening, exploring the gift.

She blinked, shutting him out, and pointed upward. "See that nest? It has little birds in it. God taught each bird how to take care of the hatchlings. Do you think He cares any less about us?" She cupped her hands. "I think He holds us gently in His palms."

It was a picture he wished he could believe. "What about when we disobey Him? Does He throw us away?"

"He holds us closer." She closed her hands, as if holding something precious, and brought them to her chest, next to her heart. Then turned her face up to him. She smiled so gently, so joyfully, that his chest felt ready to explode. Oh, if only his faith could be so pure. So simple.

He was not a simple man. Could never revert to a way of living such as the natives enjoyed—hunting, fishing, living by the seasons. Life was far more complicated in his world. However, he considered himself a fair man, and there was one more thing he must do to be fair. "I would like you to help me at the clinic." The words were easier to say than he anticipated.

Teena stared at him knowing all her joy showed in her face, naked and overwhelming. She did not care. God had answered her prayer. If she'd been alone she would have fallen on her knees and thanked her Heavenly Father. Instead, she smiled and nodded. "I will help you. You will help me."

He looked ready to argue, then smiled. "We'll work together."

It was all she could do not to dance the rest of the way to the clinic. When she saw Annabelle watching them her joy sagged, her feet lagged. Would she be forced to work with the woman?

Jacob noticed her pause. "I thought you were anxious to do this."

She squared her shoulders. If that's what it took, she would do it. "I am."

Jacob's boots thudded on the boardwalk. The safe distance narrowed, until she had only one more step before she'd be in the clinic yard and face-to-face with the woman who shot her a look fit to tan leather. Jacob ground to a halt. His shoulders tensed as he faced Annabelle. "We need to talk."

Teena ducked her head and slipped away to the far side of the building. She did not want to hear his explanation as to why she was going to help. She would spare herself more of Annabelle's angry glare.

"Teena." It was Dr. Jacob.

Stilling her anxious feet to a calm pace, she went to him.

"Where did you disappear to?"

She shrugged.

"Never mind. Let's get to work. First I'll show you how to clean the instruments."

Although she already knew from watching him teach Annabelle, she let him explain the procedure again.

"It will be an easier task, once the big stove is set up in the clinic."

"Much cooler outside." Seems it would cook the patients as well as the instruments to have a hot stove inside.

He straightened. "I suppose it is. But the rain—"

"Make a roof of canvas."

He chuckled. "Of course. Why didn't I think of it?"

She resisted the urge to point out white men tended to complicate things far more than necessary.

"You're right. Seems I too often make things more complicated than they need to be."

She stared at him. How had he guessed at her thoughts? "I did not say that."

His grin made her insides laugh. "You don't always hide your thoughts as well as you think."

She flashed a smile, somehow not minding that this man had read her mind.

They spent a happy half hour cleaning instruments and boiling them.

"Can I ask a question?" So many things burned at her thoughts, but she dared not ask them all.

"By all means. You won't learn if you don't ask."

"That liquid in the brown bottle—"

"The laudanum I use for pain relief. What about it?"

"Do you make it?"

"No, I buy it."

"Who makes it? How is it made? What is it?"

He chuckled. "One question, huh?" He grew thoughtful. "I could probably make my own laudanum. It's a tincture—" He paused, and when he resumed he spoke slowly. "Made from poppy pods." He seemed reluctant to say more, but she burned with a desire to know.

"What is a poppy?"

"A flower. A plant."

Her eyes felt as wide as her mouth, which had fallen open. "White men use the same methods?" It was beyond belief.

He scrubbed his hand over his face and sighed deeply. "I have been very blind, as Margie so kindly told me.

Yes, we use plants. The only difference is…" He looked confused. "I was going to say we do it scientifically. How narrow-minded is that?" He shook his head. "Come, I'll teach you about dressings."

She followed him into the clinic, bracing herself for Annabelle's glare. But she didn't see her, and stopped to assess the situation. Where was the woman? Better an enemy in the open than one in hiding.

"What's wrong," Jacob asked.

"I don't see Annabelle."

"She won't be back."

Margie roared her approval. "About time you opened your eyes. Now, what about the lineup of men out there?"

Jacob laughed. "Hang on. I'll tell them Annabelle will no longer be helping me. My guess is, by the time I'm done here the numbers will be greatly reduced."

Teena turned her back to the others in the room as Jacob went out to make his announcement. She could not let them see her face and guess how honored she was to be chosen to help Jacob. Above Annabelle. To feel like he approved of her.

She tried to still the eager excitement churning up her insides. Told herself it was only because she was achieving her goal of learning the white man's ways— but it was more. More than joy that God had heard and answered her prayer. It was rooted in the knowledge she would be working with Jacob. Watching his compassion as he treated the sick and injured, observing his healing hands, hearing his deep voice that called to deep places in her heart.

"You cannot be a white woman." Jimmy's words echoed through her head but did not quench the way her heart yearned toward Jacob. She knew she should end such foolish thoughts. Knew she would become intimately acquainted with soul-wrenching pain if she allowed them to continue. Yes, Jacob had changed enough to be willing to teach her how to be a white man's nurse. But she knew in her mind there could be nothing more. Too bad her heart did not listen to reason.

He was right about the lines dwindling with Annabelle's departure. In two days, only a handful stood waiting for the doctor to see them, and those who did had real need of medical attention.

Teena's heart almost spilled over with joy at being at Jacob's side and watching him work. Learning he listened to the heart and lungs with the stethoscope.

"You listen." He held the earplugs toward her.

"Get away," the big scruffy man said. "No Injun is listening to my chest. I'd as soon die of whatever is wrong."

Jacob straightened and backed away. "Suit yourself."

Scruffy looked surprised. "Doc, you mean you ain't gonna treat me?"

"Don't see how I can if you won't allow my nurse to assist me."

Teena felt suspended over the deepest gorge in the mountains as her emotions warred with reason. Jacob had defended her. Made her feel accepted in a way she had never felt outside her clan. But he couldn't afford to offend his white patients. Word would get around and people would stay away. Perhaps choose to die uncared for, as this man threatened.

Scruffy shuffled his feet, twisted his hat. "Can't you help me without having her here?"

"I'm afraid not."

Neither man budged.

Teena began to back away. "I will leave."

"You will stay," Jacob said in a voice that allowed no argument.

Scruffy relented first. "All right." He opened his shirt. "Have a listen. I can always have me a good soak in the river afterwards."

"Don't think it would do you any harm," Jacob murmured and turned his attention to Teena, not giving the man a chance to defend himself.

Teena heard the sigh of air and knew it was the man's lungs working. Jacob moved the stethoscope and she heard clearly the *thumpa-thump* of the man's heart. She listened a moment longer then lifted her head. "It's amazing." She and Jacob shared a flash of mutual wonderment and something more…something transcending medicine, healing instruments or anything visible. She shared the same hopes, desires, yearnings and, yes, even disappointments, though she didn't know the exact shape and size of his disappointment. Couldn't even name hers in this fragile, fleeting sliver of time.

"Ain't you gonna have a listen, Doc?"

Jacob took the stethoscope and bent over the man.

For a heartbeat, two and another, Teena lingered in the beauty of the moment.

Later, alone, she pulled out the tiny scene and considered it, reshaping it and examining it. How easy it would be to turn it into a tale to share on the long winter nights. How that small, almost nonexistent bit of time had become the beginning of something bigger.

The enormity of where her heart had led her thoughts hit her, and she sprang to her feet. *Siteen Crow, you are a silly dreamer. You are a Tlingit. All you want from Jacob is to learn his ways. And all he wants from you is...*

Nothing. He wanted nothing from her. Wouldn't even have chosen her to help him if Annabelle had shown a pinch of sense.

She had come to the forest to gather leaves and roots of the season, but instead had idled away the better part of the afternoon with dreaming. Now she had to work at a furious pace to make up for lost time.

Lana Tanner decided the new clinic required a formal opening celebration. Mack could deny his wife nothing and agreed.

Jacob saw no need for such an event, but Lana would not take no for an answer. Jacob had watched in amazement as she oversaw the organization of his belongings into an orderly fashion he hadn't imagined possible. Though he wondered how he would ever locate anything in the future. Even the tent, which he now shared with Burns, who had recovered completely and spent as much time on the beach, or fishing, as possible, had been tidied beyond recognition.

Jacob was too busy, too content with the way things settled into a routine to pay much mind to it, other than to waste half an hour trying to locate a book he'd left by his bed.

Teena had turned out to be a quick learner. He could ask her to examine a patient, and she did so quietly and efficiently, often able to tell him exactly the person's ailment. Yes, she'd had experience with illness, but still, her skill amazed him.

She was a joy to work with, too. Many times, she anticipated what he needed even before he did. It was like having an extra right arm at his disposal.

But that wasn't all that pleased him. It was the moments when their eyes met and he felt a silent connection, an unspoken communication that gave him a rush of amazement. He couldn't say exactly what it was he felt. Only that it was good.

He'd taught her to stitch cuts, bandage wounds and administer laudanum. And so much more. He had no qualms about leaving her in charge of the clinic when he was called away.

"Jacob." Mack's call brought Jacob's attention back to the festivities around him. "Come over here."

Lana had organized a formal greeting line and Jacob was expected to be in it. He first sought out the young woman who filled so much of his thoughts. "Teena, join me."

She drew back. "I don't think I should."

"Why not? You're an official part of this clinic."

"I am Tlingit."

"Mack and Lana wouldn't object." He hated that he couldn't say the same for everyone else gathered. And where had all these people come from? All dressed up in their best finery, but some with prejudice dirtying their minds.

Mack joined Jacob. "Lana is waiting."

"I'm trying to convince Teena she should join us."

Mack grabbed Teena's hand. "Of course she should."

A look of fear crossed Teena's face so quickly, Jacob could almost make himself believe he hadn't seen it. Almost. Wanting to reassure her, he pulled her free hand through his arm.

As soon as Mack saw they were on their way, he hurried back to Lana's side.

Jacob murmured, "You're safe with me. I won't let anyone hurt you."

She giggled. "I'm not afraid of being attacked. After all, have you seen Jimmy? My brother would deal with anyone who hurt me."

"Physically, yes. But does he protect your feelings against what people say?"

She shot him a look of pure amazement. "You think you can do that?"

He chuckled. "I'll try."

Her eyes darkened and she shook her head. "I don't want you to."

Her words stung. He wanted to guard her from people's cruelty. Thought saying so would make her realize he had grown to care for her. "Why not?"

"You are white. I am Tlingit. That's all anyone will ever see. If you don't accept that, you will offend many people."

He wanted to argue, but they had reached the lineup and he could not say more. Couldn't tell her there had to be something else. A bridge that crossed the barrier.

Lana introduced people, taking his mind from the quandary. Many of those presented he had already met at church, in the store, on the street or even in the clinic. He accepted their thanks and congratulations on the modern medical facilities. Teena stayed by his side. She spoke to those who spoke to her, and drew back as if wanting to disappear at those who ignored her. Jacob understood her presence in the greeting line signaled acceptance from Mack—"Mr. Treasure Creek," as Lana teasingly called him—and prevented many from speaking their minds that an Indian should have such an honor.

Teena waited until Lana invited everyone to join them for tea and cake before she slipped away. Jacob's offer to protect her would be stored with the other memories for her to cherish and enjoy privately in the future.

She stared to where the trail entered the trees. She'd escape to her village, except Jacob watched her and she knew he would come after her and stop her. She felt his eyes on her as she moved among the crowd, and had only to look across the distance to meet his gaze.

She overheard bits and pieces of conversation. It seemed everything was about gold. Did these people value nothing else—like family, traditions, the land? She had only to glance about to know the answer to the last question. They had turned the beach to a sea of mud stinking with their garbage. The once pure, peaceful Chilkoot Trail was now a trail of anger and greed, strewn with the white man's discards.

She edged away from the talk of gold, only to hear it from another set of lips.

"There's sixty gold nuggets buried around here," a shrill voice whispered.

At least Teena suspected he considered it a whisper, but if not for the noise of so many people, his voice would have carried to the waterfront. She paused, out of sight behind the tent where Jacob and Burns slept, wondering why the man thought there was so much gold buried.

"Who'd bury gold? What good is that?" The second voice sounded as young and excited as the first.

"Sure would be easier digging it up than crossing those mountains."

"Yeah, but how would we know where to dig?"

"Must be a map. Don't all buried treasures have one?"

The other person laughed without humor. "Yeah, and

I guess we'd find one posted in the store for everyone to see."

"There's gotta be clues somewhere." The speaker didn't disguise an injured tone. "I'm going to see if'n I can find them. I aim to find that gold."

As she moved on she glanced to the side, where two young fellows about Burns's age crowded close, as if keeping a secret. Teena shook her head. They should be home helping their family. Instead, they chased after gold. Nonexistent gold, if they thought to find buried gold nuggets.

"That's her." Another voice from a different direction hit Teena's ears and she turned to see who had caused such awe in the speaker's voice. It was Viola Goddard.

"She has the baby. Heard it was Indian."

There were those who thought it might be Tlingit because of the moccasins she wore, but despite the dark hair, Teena knew this was no Tlingit baby.

"I hear they're looking for the baby's family."

Viola pulled every man's eyes in her direction as she moved toward Lana. Seems white men liked a woman with hair the color of red berries.

"You know the baby is worth its weight in gold."

"How so?"

"Whoever dropped it off left gold to provide for its care."

"How much gold?"

Teena did not understand these people. Was gold the only thing that mattered?

"I heard it was the weight of the baby."

"What does a baby weigh? Six, ten pounds, at least. Right? Maybe more. Why, I think I could look after that baby pretty good for twelve nuggets of gold. I might be the father. You never know." They laughed mockingly.

Teena shifted so she could see who spoke. A man darkened by the sun, with lanky, black hair, and a smaller, paler man. She could tell them they didn't stand a chance of claiming that baby. Others had tried and failed. Mack and Sheriff Parker weren't fooled by pretend family.

Jacob suddenly appeared at her elbow. "Are you enjoying yourself?"

"Some."

"You didn't get a piece of cake, so I brought you one." He handed her a thick slice on a china plate.

"Thank you." She'd avoided the food line, knowing her presence bothered some of those present, even if they would guard their tongues with Mack and Lana standing nearby.

Jacob glanced about. "I thought Jimmy might come, but I haven't seen him."

"You won't."

Jacob brought his gaze back to Teena. His expression was thoughtful. "Has he got something against associating with a white man?"

How could he be so stubbornly blind, especially when it wasn't so long ago he viewed her with the same suspicion? "No more so than they have with associating with him."

"But he's one of the best packers."

"He is." *Just as I am one of the most respected healers, and you didn't accept it.*

"What we need is a bridge between the natives and the white people."

A bridge. The word had come to her thoughts once or twice. "What would such a bridge look like?"

His smile was weary, self-mocking. "I have no idea." His attention shifted toward the clinic. "Margie is still with Thad. She doesn't think he'll survive if she doesn't watch him day and night."

Frankie had stomped over from the church, almost stumbled when she saw Lucy at Caleb's side in a very pretty dress. Maybe it was the same one she wore to church. Teena couldn't say. But if she wasn't mistaken, Frankie was surprised and perhaps a bit disgruntled to see her sister looking so pretty. She overheard her mumble close to Lucy's ear, "You'll always be a Tucker."

Lucy had smiled sweetly.

Jacob continued on toward the clinic. "I'm going to send Margie out."

"Let me do it."

He nodded, and Teena hurried to relieve the other woman, glad of a chance to get away from the crowd.

He was right about Margie. She left every day, only to attend to work. She'd finished the exterior of the clinic and now helped Frankie and Lucy work on the church, yet she still managed to spend a great deal of time at Thad's bedside. "I hate to think how I would feel, strapped to a bed and forced to lay still," she said, when Jacob commented.

Teena told Margie the doctor wanted her to join the celebration. Margie let out a blast of air that stirred the covers on Thad's bed. "Ain't got much use for all that fake smilin'."

"The cake is good." Teena finished her piece. "Do you mind taking the plate back?"

Thad eyed the empty plate. "I wouldn't mind a piece of cake."

Margie lumbered to her feet. "I'll get you some. But I don't intend to chitchat with those out there."

Thad chuckled. "Why would you, when you can enjoy my scintillating company?"

Margie's face reddened to the roots of her hair. "Don't give yourself much credit, do you?" She stomped from the room, Thad's pleased chuckle following her.

He turned to Teena. "I'll be fine on my own."

She knew that to be so. Despite Margie's protests, Jacob often left him alone and insisted Margie didn't need to be at his bedside continually. "I prefer your company, too."

He chuckled. "My head is going to get so swelled I'll need more pillows to hold it."

She had no idea what he meant, but smiled. Outside, the noise of the crowd rumbled like a nearby river, but inside was quiet and peaceful.

* * *

Jacob watched for Teena to return, even though he suspected she wouldn't. Did she really feel as ostracized by white people as she said? He'd gotten so used to her presence, he found it hard to believe. Perhaps she couldn't read or write, but then likely, thousands climbing the Chilkoot Trail also could not. Certainly, she was as intelligent as any woman he'd known, and a lot brighter than some. Memories of working with Annabelle flitted across his mind. What a contrast between the two.

Mack called him and Jacob spent the next hour answering greetings. By the time the crowd had dispersed and Mack and Lana arranged for the tables and party stuff to be removed, Jacob had had his fill of socializing. As soon as he could, he headed for the clinic.

Inside, Margie and Thad laughed at a shared joke.

Teena was not there.

"She went home to look after her father." Margie supplied the answer to a question he didn't ask.

"Of course. And shouldn't you be going home, too?"

The look she gave him made him glad he stood a distance away. "You telling me to leave?"

He sighed. "I'm only suggesting you should get your rest."

"Fine."

He didn't move, uncertain what to do. For the first time since his arrival, he had no patients needing his attention.

* * *

He managed to make it through the day without anyone demanding to know why his brow was so furrowed. He did not sleep well that night. Who could sleep when it was always light out? Only, he'd been sleeping just fine until now. He rose early and decided to do an inventory of his supplies.

"Jacob, Jacob."

At Burns's anxious cry, the task was forgotten. "What is it?"

"Someone needs your help."

"I'll be right there." He hurried outside. A young man he recognized from the opening celebration stood beside Burns, his eyes wide, his lips trembling, his face streaked as if he'd been crying. Was he the emergency? Apart from his mental distress he seemed sound. Jacob looked about for an injured person. "Who needs me?"

"Tell him," Burns prodded the young fellow.

"He's up there." He pointed to the Chilkoot. "He fell."

"On some rocks?" Jacob had seen a number of injuries from such falls—cuts, sprained ankles, a couple of head injuries like Emery Adams, one of his first patients.

The quivering lad shook his head. "Off the mountain."

"Off?" Jacob remembered the vistas he'd seen on the trail. "Where is he now?"

"Still there. I couldn't get to him."

Jacob's mind raced with possibilities. Hanging on

the side of a cliff. Facedown in the river. Body broken, bleeding. "Burns, run and tell Mack."

Burns dashed away.

Jacob grabbed his doctor's bag, checked to make sure it contained all he needed, then paused. The lad stood shaking like a sapling in a strong wind. "Sit down. Take a deep breath and tell me what happened." Even as the boy spoke, Jacob tried to think what would be required for a rescue, but he needed more information in order to plan. If only he knew the area better. He'd have to trust Mack's knowledge.

"What's your name, son?"

"Pete. Peter Neilson." He sucked in air and released it in a rush of words. "I told him the gold wouldn't be there, but he saw this stack of rocks and said it marked a special spot. Likely the buried gold. So we started to move the rocks. One got stuck. It was big, you know. Martin said he could get it from the far side." The boy shuddered. "The rock rolled his way and took him over the cliff."

"Could you see him?" Was he crushed beneath the rock? If so, Jacob didn't hold out much hope for him.

Peter couldn't speak. His eyes wide enough to swallow his head, he managed a nod.

"Could you tell if he was breathing?"

A shake of his head.

"Did you see blood?"

Another shake of his head.

Teena stepped into view. He tried to tell himself his relief at seeing her was because she knew the trail.

She'd be able to help. Yes, he was relieved she was here to assist with the fallen man, but more—much, much more—he was glad she had come back to him. *To help him,* he corrected. He turned his attention back to Peter, lest Teena see his expression and guess his feelings.

She must never know how he felt. It would make the situation uncomfortable for both of them. They belonged in different worlds. He in Seattle; she here.

His emotions firmly under lock and key, he signaled to her, guessed from the look on her face she had heard enough to know what was going on.

Peter shuddered so hard his teeth rattled. "His arm was real crooked."

"Do you have family here?"

The boy's expression saddened and he hung his head. "My ma and pa."

"Where are they?"

He pointed to a spot on the beach.

Mack and Burns rushed toward them. Mack had a coil of rope over his shoulder and a pack over his back. Jacob sent Burns to notify the family and tell them to wait at the clinic with Peter, then he and Mack discussed what they would need.

Teena knelt before the distraught boy, asking him how far up the trail they'd gone. The boy didn't know. But he described the setting.

She straightened. "I know where it is. I'll show you."

Mack nodded. "Let's do it."

She led the way up the trail, setting a brutal pace that covered the distance in a hurry. Jacob was soon panting, but none of them slowed. Time was of the essence.

However, he wondered if Teena could keep up her pace. As if reading his mind, she glanced over her shoulder and flashed a smile at him. His heart responded in a way both strange and familiar—familiar as the comforts of home, the pleasure of a hot, sweet cup of tea after a hard day's work, as refreshing as a golden sunrise. But the way his heart and mind and soul sought something more than comfort in her smile was something new, too raw to allow him to identify it. He barred the door to such thoughts.

The trail grew more challenging and he forced his attention to what they might find ahead.

He lost track of time as he concentrated on his breathing and following Mack.

"Here," Teena called. "It's near here."

They'd covered a great distance and all of them sucked in great gulps of air. Jacob tried to estimate how long they'd been on the trail. It had been too long. The fallen boy could have succumbed to his injuries.

Teena pointed to a pile of rocks.

This must be the spot. He hurried to the edge and glanced over. The boy lay on a ledge below, his arm bent at an awkward angle. Broken. From here he saw no blood. A good sign.

Teena and Mack were at his side, studying the situation.

Margie studied him. "We ordered supper from the restaurant."

He didn't ask if they'd ordered enough for three. Seems they wanted him to leave them alone. "I'll get a bite to eat later." With that, he backed away. The pair inside resumed a raucous conversation as soon as he was out of sight. Something about a time Margie roped a cow and was yanked off her feet. Thad chuckled. Jacob was glad Margie kept Thad entertained. A restless patient could be difficult.

He stopped on the rough sidewalk and studied his surroundings, seeing the crowds of people as if from a vast distance. It wasn't that he felt left out. Or lonely. He simply wasn't used to being at loose ends.

He looked toward the Indian village with a great longing to talk to Teena. There was something he wanted to say, but he didn't even know what it was. He forced his feet to head in the opposite direction. Even if he knew what he ached to say, Teena's father would most certainly not welcome a visit from him.

Surely, he could find someone on the trail needing him.

He found a man with a cut that needed cleaning, another with a rash for which he offered some ointment. But nothing serious. Nothing truly demanding his attention.

So he climbed higher, letting his thoughts push in and out with each breath. Something inside him had shifted. He didn't know what or why or when. The trail grew steeper, more rocky. He came to a spot reminding him of Teena's story. Her white friend had been injured by a large rock such as one of these. Teena might have grown bitter. Blamed God. Instead, she drew closer to God. Saw Him in bits and pieces of nature. He supposed it came from her connection with the elements. But would he have responded the same way, given the same circumstances?

He sat and studied the water tumbling below him and tried to sort out his jumbled thoughts. After a futile hour, he pushed to his feet and turned toward Treasure Creek. All he could conclude was this place was so different from Seattle he couldn't think straight.

The sooner he returned to the city and his normal way of life, the sooner his world would again make sense. He'd put all this behind him and forget it.

Except he knew he would never forget Treasure Creek, nor the satisfaction of building a suitable clinic in a rough-and-tumble place. He'd never forget the people he met here. Nor the cross section of humanity— desperate people for the most part. Some good. Some not so good.

There was much he would not forget.

Most of all, he knew he would never forget Teena and how her quiet, gentle presence had eased his stubborn prejudice aside.

The next day was quiet, and at noon he told Teena she might as well leave. Not because he wanted her to, but because all day, no matter what his hands were doing, his thoughts circled back to her. He mentally listed her attributes. Besides being efficient and a quick learner, besides being beautiful as any woman he'd ever met, she had an aura about her that spoke of peace and serenity. It intrigued him. Beckoned to him. Enticed his thoughts down pathways drawing him away from his carefully constructed plans.

His plans suddenly seemed less developed than he thought. He wasn't as certain of who he was and what he wanted as he once believed himself to be.

With a mutter of disgust, he pushed back from the desk where he attempted to make notes of his work. Attempted and failed.

"Something wrong, Doc?" Margie called from the next room, where she had brought her lunch to share with Thad.

Nothing she would understand. How she'd chuckle if she knew how Teena had burrowed into his thoughts. "I'm going to see if I have any mail." He grabbed his hat and strode toward Duncan MacDougal's place. MacDougal served as jack-of-all-trades—smithy, postmaster and even jailer when the need arose, having fashioned a makeshift cell in the back of his shop.

Twenty feet from his destination, his steps slowed. Teena paused at the entrance to Tanner's General Store. He hesitated, not sure what to do…hurry to her side or continue on his way? His uncertainty twisted through him, a flint that sparked a meager anger. When had he ever been so confused about anything, let alone about a woman?

She stepped inside and immediately backed out, a burly man in her face.

Even from where he stood, Jacob heard every insulting, dirty word.

Two men joined the first, almost surrounding Teena. One jabbed at her shoulder. Another gave one of her braids a root-tearing jerk.

"Stop." Jacob leaped forward. "I have never seen such appalling behavior." He swallowed the bitter taste on the back of his tongue as he closed the distance between himself and the tormenting trio.

The three turned in unison, matching scowls upon their faces.

"Yeah? What are you? An Indian lover?" The bigger one leaned close, trying to intimidate Jacob.

Jacob refused to be moved by the man's size and belligerence. "I'm a respecter of humankind."

"Nah." One of the smaller men leered in Jacob's face. "You just think you can have that sweet little thing all to yourself." His laughter rang with wicked mockery. Then he added a few off-color comments.

Jacob turned to apologize to Teena, but she had slipped away, disappeared. He steamed away, his thoughts raging, his brain seething. How could people be so ignorant? So cruel? Teena did not deserve such treatment. The sound of his boots clattering on the boards echoed through his head. He tried to concentrate on the noise, hoping it would make the confusion of his thoughts fade away. But he could not stop thinking of Teena. How he'd wanted to rescue her. How his heart ached for her torment.

She led the way up the trail, setting a brutal pace that covered the distance in a hurry. Jacob was soon panting, but none of them slowed. Time was of the essence.

However, he wondered if Teena could keep up her pace. As if reading his mind, she glanced over her shoulder and flashed a smile at him. His heart responded in a way both strange and familiar—familiar as the comforts of home, the pleasure of a hot, sweet cup of tea after a hard day's work, as refreshing as a golden sunrise. But the way his heart and mind and soul sought something more than comfort in her smile was something new, too raw to allow him to identify it. He barred the door to such thoughts.

The trail grew more challenging and he forced his attention to what they might find ahead.

He lost track of time as he concentrated on his breathing and following Mack.

"Here," Teena called. "It's near here."

They'd covered a great distance and all of them sucked in great gulps of air. Jacob tried to estimate how long they'd been on the trail. It had been too long. The fallen boy could have succumbed to his injuries.

Teena pointed to a pile of rocks.

This must be the spot. He hurried to the edge and glanced over. The boy lay on a ledge below, his arm bent at an awkward angle. Broken. From here he saw no blood. A good sign.

Teena and Mack were at his side, studying the situation.

She'd be able to help. Yes, he was relieved she was here to assist with the fallen man, but more—much, much more—he was glad she had come back to him. *To help him,* he corrected. He turned his attention back to Peter, lest Teena see his expression and guess his feelings.

She must never know how he felt. It would make the situation uncomfortable for both of them. They belonged in different worlds. He in Seattle; she here.

His emotions firmly under lock and key, he signaled to her, guessed from the look on her face she had heard enough to know what was going on.

Peter shuddered so hard his teeth rattled. "His arm was real crooked."

"Do you have family here?"

The boy's expression saddened and he hung his head. "My ma and pa."

"Where are they?"

He pointed to a spot on the beach.

Mack and Burns rushed toward them. Mack had a coil of rope over his shoulder and a pack over his back. Jacob sent Burns to notify the family and tell them to wait at the clinic with Peter, then he and Mack discussed what they would need.

Teena knelt before the distraught boy, asking him how far up the trail they'd gone. The boy didn't know. But he described the setting.

She straightened. "I know where it is. I'll show you."

Mack nodded. "Let's do it."

the side of a cliff. Facedown in the river. Body broken, bleeding. "Burns, run and tell Mack."

Burns dashed away.

Jacob grabbed his doctor's bag, checked to make sure it contained all he needed, then paused. The lad stood shaking like a sapling in a strong wind. "Sit down. Take a deep breath and tell me what happened." Even as the boy spoke, Jacob tried to think what would be required for a rescue, but he needed more information in order to plan. If only he knew the area better. He'd have to trust Mack's knowledge.

"What's your name, son?"

"Pete. Peter Neilson." He sucked in air and released it in a rush of words. "I told him the gold wouldn't be there, but he saw this stack of rocks and said it marked a special spot. Likely the buried gold. So we started to move the rocks. One got stuck. It was big, you know. Martin said he could get it from the far side." The boy shuddered. "The rock rolled his way and took him over the cliff."

"Could you see him?" Was he crushed beneath the rock? If so, Jacob didn't hold out much hope for him.

Peter couldn't speak. His eyes wide enough to swallow his head, he managed a nod.

"Could you tell if he was breathing?"

A shake of his head.

"Did you see blood?"

Another shake of his head.

Teena stepped into view. He tried to tell himself his relief at seeing her was because she knew the trail.

* * *

He managed to make it through the day without anyone demanding to know why his brow was so furrowed. He did not sleep well that night. Who could sleep when it was always light out? Only, he'd been sleeping just fine until now. He rose early and decided to do an inventory of his supplies.

"Jacob, Jacob."

At Burns's anxious cry, the task was forgotten. "What is it?"

"Someone needs your help."

"I'll be right there." He hurried outside. A young man he recognized from the opening celebration stood beside Burns, his eyes wide, his lips trembling, his face streaked as if he'd been crying. Was he the emergency? Apart from his mental distress he seemed sound. Jacob looked about for an injured person. "Who needs me?"

"Tell him," Burns prodded the young fellow.

"He's up there." He pointed to the Chilkoot. "He fell."

"On some rocks?" Jacob had seen a number of injuries from such falls—cuts, sprained ankles, a couple of head injuries like Emery Adams, one of his first patients.

The quivering lad shook his head. "Off the mountain."

"Off?" Jacob remembered the vistas he'd seen on the trail. "Where is he now?"

"Still there. I couldn't get to him."

Jacob's mind raced with possibilities. Hanging on

Chapter Eight

Teena understood the dangers. She could be dashed against the rocks as she descended, or the rope might give out, or…

She would not think of the risks. Only of the boy below waiting for rescue. "I'm ready," she said again, heading for the edge. Her life was in the hands of these men—all white men. They must hold the rope and lower her by brute strength, and then pull her up again. She smiled. "Good thing I don't weigh as much as my Auntie Mae."

Jacob didn't even smile. His silent message reached her mind. *I don't want you to go. I don't want you to take this risk.*

But she must. She was the best one to do it.

Thomas jerked off his hat. "Before we do this, let's pray for safety." He reached for Jacob's hand on one side, Mack's on the other.

Jacob reached for her hand.

She hesitated. Wanted to refuse, but Thomas was ready to pray. She brushed her hand to Jacob's but he gripped it firmly, silently signaling his concern. His touch swept up her arm and flooded her body. As quickly as the sensation came, it withdrew to a pool of sundrenched quicksilver in the depths of her heart.

Thomas prayed for Teena's safety and the well-being of the young man below. After his "Amen," they all stood silent and united, then Teena broke away. Her hand was cold and small. But the warmth in her heart remained like something solid and permanent.

She edged toward the rim; the shale skittered away, sending a rain of rocks downward. "If I loosen a rock on the way down it could hurt Martin." She moved to the right. "Let me down here." The overhang was larger, so that she could no longer see the ledge. She would have to find a way of pulling herself inward to the face of the cliff, once she was down.

Jacob held the rope, his hand close to her body, keeping her solidly on the edge, anchoring her thoughts on the memory of his touch. "Teena, don't take any risks. If you can't get him, let us pull you back up."

Their eyes locked. Somewhere deep inside she felt a fierce sensation of both pleasure and pain. Pleasure at his concern. Pain at how futile it was to care about this man. She shifted her caring to the boy below. "I will get him."

"You don't have to prove anything to me or anyone else."

"No, I don't." She backed toward the edge as the men

opened it now and held a tiny bottle of laudanum toward Martin. "Drink this."

His eyes registering both fear and pain, he swallowed the liquid.

"I'm going to have to get you on this stretcher to get you up to the top."

He turned to his left. "I can't see anything but space. How far to the ground?"

She didn't look. "Too far." Rescue from below would take too long.

"I don't think I can move enough to help you." His breathing was harder.

"Let me worry about that." She sounded calm and assured, but inside she had the same concern. There wasn't room to move him one inch either way. She glanced upward. Jacob watched her. Even from this distance she could see his worry. He shook his head. She understood his meaning. It was too dangerous to maneuver him. "Throw down another rope," she called.

Jacob disappeared from sight.

Teena suddenly felt alone and lost. He was still up there. He and Mack and Thomas. She could hear them talking. Still, she wished she could see him. It made her feel safer.

"Here you go." Jacob lowered the rope slowly, as if he didn't want any sudden movement to put Teena and Martin at risk.

"What are you going to do?" Martin's voice was shrill.

"Get you out of here." She grabbed the end of the

rope. The laudanum would help, but any movement would be agony for Martin. But there was no point in delaying. Every passing second made his condition more precarious. "I'm going to make a harness around you with this rope, then hold you while they lift us out."

He groaned.

"I'll be as gentle as possible, but I won't pretend it won't hurt."

"Me neither."

"Here we go." She had to almost crawl on top of him to ease the rope under him. The color left his face. "Don't pass out yet," she murmured. Once he was in position, it would be the best possible thing, but not until then.

She pulled a length between his legs to create a harness that would put less strain on his back than a simple loop around the waist. She made sure the knots were secure. "I need another foot of rope for me," she called to Jacob. He signaled to the others, and she was suddenly without the security of a taut rope. She ignored the way her heart clambered up her throat. "You are going to have to hold tight to me as they lift us."

"My arm."

"I'll hold it as best I can."

"It's gonna hurt."

She nodded. "I'm afraid so. Are you man enough to take it?"

He looked ready to cry, but at her question he swallowed hard. "I'm man enough." His determination faltered as she lowered herself along his body.

"Hold on to me."

He lifted his good arm. She slipped her arms under his back. Doing her best to ignore his groans—though they reverberated from his chest to hers—she pressed the broken arm to his side and held it firmly. "Lift us up."

"Hang on," Jacob called down.

The rope tightened about her waist. She knew the moment it took Martin's weight, as a groan escaped from deep inside him.

"I'm sorry," he managed to squeeze out. "I don't feel much like a man."

"You're doing well. Your mother would be proud of you."

"Teena, we'll lift you slowly. Here you come." Jacob's voice guided her. She held on to each word as they inched upward. Martin was a deadweight, and she suspected he had passed out. Best thing for him.

The rope twisted and she banged against the jagged rocks, taking brutal punishment as she turned to protect Martin.

"Slower," Jacob ordered the others. "Are you okay?"

She nodded.

"Halfway," he said, his voice steady and steadying. "Watch for the rock to your left. Steady. Steady. How are you doing?"

Inch-by-inch they rose to the top. She lost track of their progress, until finally Jacob caught her and eased her over the edge, lowered her to the ground and peeled her arms off Martin. "Are you okay?"

Spent, she fell to her back and waited for her strength to return. "I'm fine. Look after Martin."

He had already turned to the boy and quickly examined him. "It's impossible to tell if he's injured inside. Let's get him to the clinic."

Mack offered a hand, and helped Teena sit up so they could take the stretcher off her back. Thomas assisted Jacob in getting Martin secured on it. They were ready for the trip down the trail.

Jacob knelt in front of Teena, where she still sat trying to find the strength to stand. "Let me look at you."

"I'm fine." Though she felt like she floated in a languid pool of water.

He took her hands and turned them over.

She stared at her palms, surprised at how bloody they were.

"As I thought. Those rocks are razor sharp." He wiped the blood away with a dampened cloth, his touch so gentle she couldn't blink her eyes for fear of spilling the moisture gathering in them. He held her hand in his warm palm.

She groped from one heartbeat to the next. Sucked in air that stuck halfway to her lungs. Tried to reason with herself. He only treated her as he would any injured person—white or Tlingit, male or female. It had no special significance.

But she felt as if the rope that lay limp between them had been secured to both their hearts and drawn tight.

He applied ointment and bound her hand with glistening white bandages. His fingers lingered on the swaddled palms. Strong, healing fingers that spoke as much about the man as his words. He raised his head and met her eyes.

She blinked back her raw feelings. Blamed the anxiety of rescuing Martin for the fluttering of her insides.

"That was an incredibly brave thing," he murmured. His eyes grew soft with things she couldn't identify. Perhaps relief, maybe gratitude, and…she dared not think she saw anything else. Slowly, almost hesitantly, he leaned forward and captured her lips in a kiss that filled her heart with a thousand promises.

She closed her eyes and let herself feel nothing but the warmth of his kiss, think nothing but the endless wishing it could mean something besides relief and gratitude.

He sat back. Said nothing.

She ducked her head, lest he see how she cherished the moment.

He squeezed her shoulder. "I hope I never see you do anything remotely like that in the future." He offered his hand to help her to her feet.

She hesitated only slightly before she lifted her arm to him. Rather than take her damaged hands, he grasped her wrist. His assistance made her feel butterfly light.

"Are you ready?"

She nodded.

Mack and Thomas carried Martin. Teena and Jacob walked on either side to steady the stretcher on the rough spots. Several times they reached for him at the same time. Even though she knew he saw her only as a fellow human being, a person to be treated kindly, given healing ministrations to—even though she understood all that, she could not contain the ruffling of her heart, as if she had swallowed a dozen butterflies who now danced inside her, light and airy and happy.

A man cried out and rushed toward them. "Martin. Martin. Is he safe?"

Jacob trotted toward the man, meeting him halfway. "Are you the boy's father?"

"Yes, I'm Mr. Neilson. Is he okay?"

"He's injured. I can't say how badly yet. We need to get him to the clinic."

"Let me help." Mr. Neilson darted over and tried to take the end of the stretcher from Mack.

Mack nudged him aside. "Let us do this. We know the trail better."

Mr. Neilson hesitated.

"You can stay with us in case we need help," Jacob said, and the man fell in behind Thomas.

Jacob focused on Martin, monitoring him for signs of internal injury. The laudanum kept him from feeling too much pain, but the sooner they got him to the clinic the better. He didn't need a crisis on the side of the mountain, or even on the treed path closer to town.

He didn't know if he could handle any more strain. The torturous minutes Teena had hung over the edge of the cliff, out of sight, his heart had refused to beat with any regularity. Three times he'd reminded himself to breathe. Thankfully, Mack and Thomas held the rope secure while Jacob hovered as close to the brink as he dared, listening for Teena. He heard her grunt once and wondered if she was hurt, suspended helplessly below him. Every time the men played out an inch of rope his skin had iced over.

Pulling her up, watching her being thumped against the rocks, had rendered him almost useless. Only his years of training and practice in remaining calm in the midst of disaster had enabled him to turn his attention to Martin first. Teena would have bruises to deal with in the coming days, but all he could do to ease her discomfort was tend to her hands.

He hadn't been able to keep from kissing her, but he wanted more. He wanted to pull her into his arms and comfort her. Comfort himself. But he didn't have the right.

"I told the boys not to go up the trail without us," Mr. Neilson said, breathless as he kept to his boy's side. "But they had some fool notion there was a fortune of gold buried up here. I told them, if there was someone else would own it. But they wouldn't listen. You know how boys are."

Thinking of Aaron, Jacob said he did.

They reached Treasure Creek and hurried to the clinic. Martin groaned with every step. A thin woman and young Peter surged forward. The woman cried freely. No doubt, Mrs. Neilson.

Her husband lifted a hand in greeting or warning. Jacob couldn't say which. "He's okay, Mother."

"My boy! My boy!" She tried to throw herself across the stretcher.

Jacob leaped forward and prevented her. "His arm is broken. You don't want to make his pain any worse, do you?"

"No. No."

The men hurried onward, Mrs. Neilson trotting beside them, weeping loudly.

He never knew how to handle a woman's tears, and glanced at Teena, silently beseeching her to help.

Teena smiled her gentle smile, which served to ease his mind considerably, then turned to Mrs. Neilson. "Please, you run ahead and see that the bed is ready for him."

"Oh, yes. I will." And she trotted away, pausing every few steps to turn and moan, "My poor boy."

A crowd soon followed on their heels, all asking questions and talking at once.

"Did they find the treasure?"

"Don't suppose they would say if they did."

"Sixty nuggets, wasn't it?"

Mack let out a harsh sound. "People, listen to me. There is no treasure. How many times do I have to tell you?"

The crowd fell back marginally, muttering about

Mack's announcement. Seemed most of them believed he only wanted to keep the treasure safely hidden.

They reached the clinic on the heels of Mrs. Neilson. Thad watched as they carried young Martin in and lifted him to the bed.

Mr. Neilson wrung his hands and his wife wept loudly.

Jacob was about to ask them to leave when Thomas spoke. "Mother, Father, can I pray with you?"

They shifted their attention to Thomas, expressions both eager and anxious.

"Let's go outside so the doctor can do his work."

They quietly accompanied him.

"He has quite the touch with people," Jacob said.

Mack nodded. "I keep telling him we need him to be the preacher for our church."

"What does he say?"

"He says he already has a mission field. He means the Tlingit and the miners on the trail. He seems to prefer his little cabin to town life, but I would sure like it if he took over the church."

They worked as they talked. Teena cut the boy's shirt off. Jacob didn't want to use ether, so he instructed Mack to hold him steady while Jacob set the arm. It was over in a moment, but not without Martin screaming once.

"Martin." Mrs. Neilson's shrill voice rent the air, followed by Thomas's calm tones.

Without being asked, Teena prepared the items for splinting.

"Your hands," he protested.

"They are fine."

He knew they weren't. They must hurt terribly. But she stood at his side, ready to assist him. He waited, his gaze on her downturned head. Not once since they'd reached the clinic had she met his eyes. In fact, he was certain she jerked away several times. "Teena?"

"Did you need something?" She kept her attention on Martin.

Yes. He needed to know what happened to the connection he'd felt up on the mountain. But what could he say? He'd overstepped the boundaries by kissing her. The best he could do now was keep his attention focused on his patient. "Let's get this young fella fixed up."

They slipped into a familiar, comfortable routine as they worked, functioning so well together there was no need for talk. He tried to tell himself nothing had changed. He almost believed it until he reached across her arm, brushing it. She didn't jerk away. In fact, she didn't even move, but he felt her stiffen.

But her reaction barely registered as an explosion rocked his insides. Something had changed in him. He didn't know what to think of it. *You don't have time to dwell on it right now. Stay focused.*

He left Teena cleaning up, and went outside to speak to the parents. "I'd like to keep him for observation."

Mrs. Neilson wrung her hands. "Is he okay?"

"So far as I can tell. Would you like to sit with him?"

She rushed for the doorway, pausing only to call, "Thank you."

"Can I...?" Mr. Neilson broke off without finishing.

"You and Peter, too. Just don't exhaust Martin."

Teena stepped outside. She stared toward the water.

He wondered what she thought of all the people gathered on the beach.

When she shuddered, he hurried to her side. "How are you feeling?"

"I am fine." Her gentle voice did not give him a clue as to how she really felt.

"No ill effects from rescuing Martin, apart from your hands?"

She didn't even bother to lift her arms and look. "I am fine."

She was *too* fine. It irked him. Couldn't she admit even a little soreness? An emotional exhaustion from the stress of the day?

Couldn't she admit she felt something toward him? Perhaps even needed some comfort from him? Instead, she developed a sudden interest in the proceedings down the street and sidled away to study them.

He wasn't fooled. She intentionally put distance between them, and his insides felt washed with vinegar. He stepped forward to face her, block her view of the street. She simply looked past him.

"Have I done something to offend you?" *Besides kiss you?*

He knew she heard by the way she twitched, but she

still refused to meet his eyes. "Teena? Why have you withdrawn?"

Her gaze jerked toward him, full of confusion. "Withdrawn? What is that?"

At least he had her attention and a chance to rekindle what they'd shared earlier in the day. He sought for a way to explain that would open a welcoming door. "Teena, I felt something up there." Without releasing her gaze he tipped his head toward the mountain. "I think you did, too."

Her eyes darkened. "I cannot. I must not." She stepped back. "I will go tend to my father." She slipped away as graceful as a shy deer. Without appearing to hurry, she quickly reached the trees and disappeared into the shadows.

She was right. Besides, he wasn't staying.

Chapter Nine

In the coming days, Jacob tried to believe nothing had changed. Martin survived his fall with only a broken arm and some nasty bruises. Jacob sent him home the next day with instructions to his mother to bring him back if anything seemed amiss. Margie continued to spend a large portion of each day with Thad. Thad's wound healed slowly; his leg would take even longer to mend. Teena assisted Jacob efficiently, eagerly learning all she could.

But something in him had changed. He denied it every morning and a thousand times throughout the day. Told himself it was only admiration for Teena's bravery. Only relief he could leave with a clear conscience, knowing someone would be ready to assist the new doctor. Of course there wasn't a new doctor yet, despite the inquiries Mack had put out.

He pushed aside his futile thoughts and turned his attention to his work. A dozen people lined up on the sidewalk to see him. Walking wounded for the most part. A few stitches, a burned arm, a rash. His biggest concern was the threat of an epidemic.

He looked at the next patient. A dark-haired young woman who perched on the edge of the chair and shifted about as if uncomfortable. "What can I do for you?"

She leaned forward. "Doctor, I'm not sick."

"Good to know. So then, what brings you here?"

She glanced about furtively. Her gaze barely registered Teena standing to one side. "I'm looking for my sister's baby."

Jacob leaned back. "How do you think I can help?"

She sighed deeply. "I figure, as the doctor, you know most everyone."

He waited for her to explain.

"You see, my sister came north with her husband and baby girl. We got word she had died and her husband was continuing on to the gold fields. Said he couldn't care for a baby on his own, so he was leaving her with someone. I've come to take her home. Poor little mite. Can you imagine losing your mama so early in life?" She sniffed and dabbed at her eyes with a handkerchief.

"Who did he leave the baby with?"

"He didn't give her full name. Just Viola. Would you know where I can find this Viola?"

Yes, he knew Viola. He also knew the furor about the baby in her care and how many had claimed to be the parent or guardian of it. Another case of chasing after fool's gold. None of what this woman said was anything but common knowledge. He would have no part in this whole nefarious business. "You're asking the wrong person for help."

She gave a little cry. "Oh, but who else can I ask? I so want to find my niece."

"You need to speak to Mack Tanner. You can normally find him at Tanner's General Store. If he isn't there, someone will be able to tell you when and where you can find him." He stood, signaling the interview was over.

She scrambled to her feet. "Thank you, Doctor. I will go find this Mr. Tanner. I pray I can find my niece soon. Poor little mite." She sniffed into her hankie as she left.

He sank to his chair and sighed. "Teena, what do you think? Is she really the aunt? Or is she looking for gold?"

Teena, still staring after the woman, slowly brought her gaze to him. "She has greed in her eyes. You people. Does nothing matter but gold?"

Her all-inclusive words stung. "We aren't all the same." Did she think greed drove him? "Are we?" He waited for her answer as if his life hung in the balance. Her opinion mattered a great deal.

She studied him, her dark eyes probing.

He let her search past his thoughts to his heart, let her examine the secret places where he seldom allowed others access.

A tender smile curved her lips and lit her eyes. "You are not like the others. You do not care about gold."

Her words were a balm to his soul, soothing rough spots of residual sorrow left from the deaths of his mother and brother; the scratch of failures and disappointments. He smiled, not caring if she saw how he felt.

She shifted her attention away, leaving him—for a heartbeat—rudderless and breathless.

"Even though you have a tin can full of gold." Her words did not accuse. She simply stated a fact. He had told her the gold would be used to buy more equipment for the clinic, perhaps to improve the tiny quarters at the far end that would serve as living area come winter. He planned to be back in Seattle by then. Who would be here? The healing balm of Teena's words lost its effectiveness. "Is there anyone else out there to see me?"

She called in the next patient. Again there hung a blanket of caution between them, as if they both realized they faced a line they could not cross.

Mack came by later. "I guess you met the woman claiming to be Goldie's aunt."

"Have you decided she isn't?"

"I thought it would be simple. Anyone knowing the baby would know some things that aren't public, but she explains she hasn't been in contact with her sister since she ran off to get married."

"So she is the aunt?"

"I can't be certain. For one thing, why doesn't she have the letter she said the father sent her? Seems she would carry it." He shrugged. "We have to have solid proof."

* * *

Teena didn't know what Mack meant by solid proof. She only knew the woman did not have love in her eyes. Only greed. She hurried down the trail toward her village. As she passed Viola's cabin, she saw her removing baby items from the drying line. She'd watched Viola with the little one. Knew she loved the baby even though it wasn't hers. There was something about Viola that made Teena's heart reach out to her. Perhaps because she wasn't quite accepted by the whites, even though she was one of them. Teena had overheard comments. Where did Viola come from? Was she running from a dreadful past? Seems people had to know all to trust. What kind of trust was that?

Viola glanced up and saw Teena watching. Teena ducked and took a step away.

"Teena, come in and have tea." Viola laughed softly. "You can join us in testing Lucy's cooking."

Teena hesitated. She didn't belong here. But Viola seemed to think otherwise. She waved her forward and waited, a basket of baby things tucked against her hip.

Viola chattered as they made their way to the door.

Teena didn't listen. Was it only Lucy inside? Lucy accepted Teena. Perhaps because she and her sisters were also different, as Margie kept saying. But if it were one of the other neighbors…some of them refused to sit on the same side of the church as the Tlingit. She hesitated at the threshold. Her air whooshed out when she saw the only other occupant besides Lucy and little Goldie was Hattie, a very kind older woman.

"I brought another person to taste your cookies," Viola announced.

Lucy turned from the oven, a large, gray apron tied about her waist. "Hi, Teena. This is what I'm making." She tipped a tray of cookies toward Teena.

Teena had had the Tuckers' offerings on more than one occasion. Hard, dry biscuits. Nothing wrong with them, but *these* were round and golden and smelled like nothing she could think of.

Hattie chuckled. "They look great, Lucy. You're a fast learner."

"Hattie is teaching me how to cook." Lucy's expression grew worried. "It's supposed to be a secret. I want to surprise Caleb and my sisters."

"I will tell no one." Teena wondered why she didn't want them to know, but it was her business who she told.

Hattie placed four pretty cups on the table. Lucy scooped the cookies to a plate. Lucy gathered the little one from the floor and sat with her on her knee.

Each of them took a cookie. Teena waited to see what the others did. Each took a bite and chewed slowly. She did the same. Oh, my. "This is nothing like any Tucker cookie I tasted. This is..." She closed her eyes and searched for a word. "Sweet and soft to the mouth."

Hattie nodded. "Good praise, I'd say."

Teena ate the cookie slowly, savoring each bite. Lucy offered her a second one. Teena took it gladly. As she ate it and enjoyed the tea, she watched how Viola nuzzled the baby and continually caressed her dark head. There was nothing but love in Viola's eyes. Not the greed she'd seen in that other woman.

"A woman asked Dr. Jacob about the baby. Said she was baby's aunt."

Viola clutched Goldie closer. "Her family?"

"She says so."

The women grew quiet. "Dr. Jacob sent her to see Mack. He asked me if I thought the woman was true."

Viola tipped her face to study Teena's expression. "What did you say?"

"I said the woman had greed in her heart. Not love. Not like the love I see in your heart."

Viola's eyes dampened. "Thank you." She choked and couldn't go on for a moment. "I pray God will protect this child from greedy people. Protect her for her real family."

Hattie and Lucy murmured agreement.

"Mack is not easily fooled," Hattie said with conviction.

Viola reached across the table and squeezed Teena's hands. "Thank you for telling me. I will pray harder."

Teena looked deep into Viola's eyes, saw not only her love for Goldie, but a yearning that drew Teena's heart to her.

"God will protect her."

She left a few minutes later, following the trail toward her village. The baby was momentarily forgotten as she recalled her conversation with Jacob. He'd wanted to know if he was like other white men. He'd been pleased when she said no.

Her heart had danced in response to his smile.

The dance fell flat as she acknowledged the truth. He wasn't like other whites, but he was still white. She dared not forget it.

Many of her clan had returned from the fishing camp and the village was busier than it had been in days. Several called greetings to her. A cousin wasn't so pleasant. "Siteen, why do you spend so much time with those people? They are a curse to us."

Another cousin joined them. "Siteen thinks she can become one of them. Some day you will learn you must choose between them and us."

The words stung. Echoed her own thoughts. She smiled. "I don't pretend I am anything but Tlingit."

"Then why spend all your time with them? Look, your father needs care. Who is preparing the winter feed for your family?"

She'd tried so often to explain why she felt it necessary to learn how to deal with white man's diseases, but so many thought the solution was simply to chase the white man from their presence. In fact, one of the other clans had burned a fort many years ago and driven away the intruders. But more came to replace them. A great tide of them. They could not be stopped. The Tlingit had to adjust to survive. Rather than explain it again, she turned to care for her father.

The next morning she returned to the clinic. Jacob had been called away to an accident at the waterfront. Margie was sitting with Thad. No one waited outside. She decided to find Jacob.

She made her way across the mud that had once been a quiet beach. She spoke English and Russian, but other languages caught her ear. Where did all these people come from?

Her eyes darted to and fro, checking out every stack of goods, noting how many people crowded around tiny tents. Two men bent over a paper. They were familiar. Together they looked up, studying the mountain as if measuring how much they could carry over the pass. They were the two from the party at the clinic. They had discussed Viola's baby. Crazy white men.

The tent flap parted and a woman stuck her head out.

Teena drew back, hiding behind a wooden crate. It was the woman who visited the clinic yesterday, claiming to be Goldie's aunt. What was she doing with the pair of men? It was proof she was lying about her relationship to the baby.

She had to tell Jacob, and rushed onward, seeking him in the melee. She located him a hundred yards farther down the beach, closing his bag. "Get the boy some clean water to drink and get off this mud hole." He glanced up, saw Teena and his face flooded with welcome.

An unsung song stuck in her heart, trying to escape into the open. He was such a good man.

His expression shifted. Grew concerned. "Teena, is there something wrong?"

Yes. But not in the way he thought. "You aren't needed at the clinic." She did not need him either.

Except to teach her how to be a nurse. How to help her people. There could never be anything more. Not so long as she was Tlingit and he was white.

"Did you want something?"

She remembered why it was so urgent to find him and speak to him. "Jacob, I saw that woman who says she is Goldie's aunt. She's with two men who were at the clinic party. I overheard them talking about the baby. They didn't know anything but what they heard. All they cared about was the gold."

"I'm sorry to hear it. I hoped the baby would find her family."

"What's wrong with Viola for family?"

"Nothing. I didn't mean that."

"Viola loves the baby."

"I know. Look, Teena, you need to tell Mack what you told me."

"I'll do so." She shifted direction. He did, too. Did he intend to accompany her to the store? She appreciated his company and didn't bother trying to explain to herself why she should.

Mack stood behind the counter of his store, writing down the supplies a young man ordered. He glanced up as Jacob and Teena stepped into the store. Must have read their expressions, because he called one of the clerks to take his place and joined them. "What's wrong?"

"Teena has something to tell you."

"Let's step into my office." He led the way.

Jacob indicated he would follow Teena. She'd seen

this gesture between the white man and woman. It seemed to signal some kind of regard. She hesitated a beat, knowing she shouldn't take the spot. She belonged walking in the white man's shadow. It never bothered her to do so. She knew who she was and didn't need to flaunt it to prove it. But he waited for her to precede him. Her heart filled with a thousand fresh blossoms, heavy with perfume. Flowers, she warned herself, were fleeting, if pleasant and enjoyable for a season.

She hurried after Mack. Jacob closed the door behind him. She had never been in this tiny room before. After all, why would a Tlingit woman be invited to such a place of honor? Most of the room was filled with a big desk. She wanted to touch it and see if each line was discernible. Most of the surface held stacks of paper, but what she could see of the top, it gleamed like oil on water. There were only two chairs, so they stood.

"What is it, Teena?"

She repeated her story. As she talked, Mack's expression darkened.

"I'm not surprised, though for a bit I wondered if this time it really was Goldie's family. Thanks for letting me know."

Teena nodded. She'd done nothing requiring thanks. To hide the truth was unthinkable.

"I'll get Ed and we'll deal with this."

Jacob and Teena returned to the clinic and the people needing to see the doctor.

As she called a man inside, she saw Mack and Sheriff Ed Parker stop in front of the tent she'd indicated.

The two men rose and an argument ensued. Then the woman lifted the canvas flap and stepped out. The argument intensified. A crowd gathered, grew agitated. "Jacob," she called into the clinic. "Could be trouble."

He joined her to watch. "Seems most of those people are itching for a good fight."

"White men are strange."

He chuckled. "I couldn't agree more. But don't the Tlingit have fights or disagreements?"

"It is not allowed within the clan. We save our anger for our enemies."

"I suppose that is part of the problem. Some of these people are enemies in the outside world. And none of them are family. Just a mass of people after gold."

"Why do they care so much for it? It can't buy happiness."

Jacob chuckled again, then grew serious. "For some it is greed. But for many others it is hope. There has been a depression in the outside world."

She did not know what the word meant.

"It means there isn't enough food. People are homeless and hungry. Finding gold will help solve those problems."

"Seems to me it only causes other problems." She pointed toward two men on the fringe of the crowd who went after each other with fists. The crowd parted to cheer on the combatants. Teena had no interest in the fight and watched Mack and the sheriff. The bigger of the two men, the dark-haired one, raised his fist and shook it in Mack's face.

"Good thing the sheriff is with him," Jacob said.

The woman wailed loud enough for Teena to hear. "Why does she cry?" There was no sorrow in her voice.

"Likely to try and convince Mack and Ed her story is true."

"But it is not." She could never understand all this trickery and falseness. "Do these people not believe in God?"

"Some do. Others only say they do."

"Why say you do if you don't?"

He considered her. "Do you always tell the truth?"

Slowly she faced him, knowing the truth required he see her eyes. "I try to."

"Even if it hurts you?"

"Even then."

"What if it hurts someone you love?" His eyes said this was more than a discussion about the value of truth. He sought to know the depth of her soul.

She opened her heart to him and let him search it, see the sincerity of her words. "I would pray for a way to speak the truth in love."

"I like that." His smile went on and on, winding through her heart, dusting off unused paths, creating trails through unfamiliar territory toward sunlit vistas.

"What's all the racket?" Margie demanded at Teena's elbow. "I could hear it over at the church. Sounds like a brawl."

Teena had forgotten the argument raging on the

beach and turned back to watch. Several more fistfights raged. The dark man and his smaller friend shouted at Mack. The woman wailed as if someone had died. Teena laughed. These people were crazy in the head but amusing.

A sudden shot startled her.

That's all they needed, men with gunshot wounds.

But it was Ed, firing into the air. Every fight ended abruptly and all eyes turned toward him.

"Enough of this. Go back to your business."

The crowd dispersed, though they didn't put a lot of distance between them and the sheriff, who now leaned close to the dark man and said something that invited no further argument. Then he and Mack strode away.

The dark man shook his fist at their backs.

"Crazy," Teena mumbled. "They're all crazy."

Margie snorted. "Ain't that the truth? Gold hunger seems to rob a man of any good sense he might have had."

"Anyone care to tell me what's going on?" Thad called. "Margie, are you out there? Have pity on a poor man and come tell me who got shot."

"Ain't nobody shot." Margie clumped into the clinic and in a loud voice, with a great deal of detail, told Thad what happened.

Jacob watched Teena leave the treed path and step to the wooden sidewalk on her journey to the clinic. Every morning he waited for her like this in his heart, if not in the doorway. As she drew closer something inside him unwound. A waiting. An expectation. He told himself over and over it was professional. Nothing more. He half believed it.

She saw him watching and her steps faltered. She glanced over her shoulder.

Did she consider returning to her village?

Not wanting to frighten her away, he turned to study the beach area. All quiet. It had been days since Mack and Ed put an end to the near riot. "I gave that trio twenty-four hours to get out of town," Ed said when he and Mack joined Jacob and Teena at the clinic. Indeed, they left on the next boat back to Skaguay. But it didn't mean the place settled into a calm holiday.

He felt Teena draw near, her footsteps barely making a sound on the sidewalk. "Good morning," he said, suddenly realizing just how good it was.

"Good morning." She stopped beside him and followed his look toward the beach. "No one broke or bleeding today?"

Yesterday had seen a rush of young men injured in a knife fight.

"Not yet. But I don't expect it will last." Then, almost as an afterthought, "I've already changed the dressings on Thad's leg."

"How does it look?"

"It's healing slowly."

She opened her mouth as if to suggest something, then closed it without speaking.

He wanted to ask her what she meant to say, but a racket to their left distracted him. Two men thumped along the wooden sidewalk, arguing loudly about the best way to get their supplies over the pass. One wanted to do it on their own. The other wanted to hire a native packer. "Faster," he insisted. "We got to get to the gold fields while there's some left to claim." They turned right and continued their journey and their argument.

"White men are crazy about gold," Teena muttered.

"White man's junk." He nodded toward the beach. "White man's diseases." His nod included the clinic. "Guess you haven't got much use for the white man." It was a question. One that consumed his insides. He knew it was foolish, but he'd deal with reality after she answered him.

Slowly she turned. Her eyes flashed, sending a thousand shards of light into his heart. She smiled, a slow release of mocking humor. "Jacob, can you honestly look around at all this—" she indicated the festering beach "—and say you're proud of being white?" She shook her head. "If these people were Tlingit, I would hang my head in disgust."

Her question startled him. She was right. On the whole, he found the conditions, the greed, the disregard for politeness and common sense beyond understanding. He grinned. "I am proud to say that lot down there is not the finest of the human race—white or otherwise."

She nodded. "On that we are agreed."

They regarded each other, sharing amusement and

regret. And something more. Something that seemed to pull them closer together.

Again he told himself he would sort out his feelings and put aside the foolish ones later. "Do you want to go with me to check the trail and see if there's anyone needing our assistance?"

She nodded.

He grabbed his bag and fell in at her side. Her ever-present pack hung on her back.

It was more like a picnic than work. They spoke to several people but saw none needing care.

"Come," she said, indicating he should follow her off the trail.

They climbed over some roots and reached a spot above the river. She sank cross-legged to the ground in a movement so fluid he wondered how she did it.

"Sit and listen."

He sat, a lot less gracefully than she had. And he listened. The sound of mankind was muted in the distance. Around him rang the sounds of nature. Birds, bees, the rustle of leaves, the rumbling of water.

"I can think here," she said, her voice blending seamlessly with the other natural sounds. "I can talk to God and listen to Him speak here." She pressed her hand to her chest. "I wish I could hear Him in the Holy Word like Mr. McIntyre did."

Jacob had a thin Bible in his bag. He always carried it. Had used it a few times to read over a dying patient. He pulled it out. "Would you like me to read to you?"

Her eyes flashed ebony light. "Would you?"

He could think of nothing else he'd rather do than spend the afternoon here, away from the crowds, alone with Teena in an atmosphere she seemed so much a part of. The Psalms suited the occasion like no other Scriptures, and he started at Chapter One. Sitting beneath trees put there by God and reading, "He shall be like a tree planted by the rivers of water," made the words alive in a way that tightened his throat.

Teena watched his mouth move with each word. Yet it did not make him self-conscious. He liked that his mouth spoke God's words to her. He read several Psalms, urged on by her silent pleading. Finally he closed the book.

She continued to study him, shifting her gaze to his nose, his ears and finally coming to stay on his eyes. Her face glowed with what he took as amazement and joy. "Thank you. I will never forget."

"I will never forget, either." He leaned closer, drawn by something he couldn't explain and didn't want to. He thought of kissing her but feared spoiling this pure moment. Instead, he closed his eyes and breathed in the aroma of the outdoors and her own unique scent. He smiled as he decided she wore the perfume of nature.

Something cracked. Perhaps only a tree dropping an old branch. But it broke the mood. They both pushed to their feet at the same time, though his rise was more of a lumbering struggle, while she rose in one movement, like someone drew her upward by an invisible string.

Neither of them spoke as they headed back down the trail toward Treasure Creek, but the silence was sweet with pleasant thoughts.

Chapter Ten

The next morning Jacob sang as he shaved. He'd promised himself to consider what had happened up the mountain with Teena. Assured himself he would think things through and be wise. Instead, he had lain awake, staring at the rough wooden walls of the clinic, with Thad sleeping nearby, and thought he had never known such a pure, unspoiled moment…such enjoyment simply in being in the company of another…as he'd felt yesterday sitting next to Teena up the mountain.

He finished his shave, brushed his hair then stepped out into a day heavy with the threat of rain. Not that it dimmed his spirits one bit.

Margie had come half an hour ago to check on Thad.

"I'm going to get breakfast," he called to her as he headed toward the restaurant. He had to wait for a place to sit, then enjoyed a hearty meal, smiling as he caught bits and pieces of conversations around him. Gold.

Where to find it. How to mine it. Where the best claims were reported. Teena was right. All that mattered to the vast majority of people here was gold.

Finished, he escaped into the open and strode toward Tanner's store. Rather than go in, he continued on to MacDougal's, on the off chance he might have some mail.

"Hey, Jacob," Duncan called. "Letter came for you. From Dawson City."

He knew no one up there. He took the letter and flicked it open.

Dr. Calloway. I saw your advertisement for a doctor in Treasure Creek. I am a doctor who thought gold would satisfy more than medical practice. I fear it has not. I'm ready to get back to medicine. Your clinic sounds ideal. May we discuss the possibility?
Your faithful servant, Dr. Andrew Bramley.

Jacob folded the page and returned it to the envelope. He'd hoped for someone to take over the clinic. He thought he'd be more excited about such a request. He stuck the letter in his pocket, to deal with later.

He left the shop and turned his steps toward the clinic, his heart swelling against his ribs as he saw Teena on the trail from the Indian village.

He waited for her at the door and allowed her to enter first. "Looks like rain," he said, and silently groaned. There were so many things he wanted to say—how was she? Was her father getting stronger? Did she enjoy working with him as much as he did with her?—and all that came out was a comment about the weather.

"I hurried to make it before the skies opened."

"Doc. Teena. Something's wrong." Margie called from the next room.

As one, they rushed to Thad's side. Jacob didn't need to check to know the man had spiked a fever. His glassy eyes and confused mumbling warned Jacob it was high. "Margie, get a basin of water and start sponging him." He ripped away the blankets and lifted the dressing. It oozed. "Infection. I hoped to avoid this. Teena, clean it. We'll use hot poultices to draw it out." He instructed her as they worked together. The poultice applied, he stepped back.

Margie continued to sponge Thad, her face wreathed in worry. "I thought he was getting better. What happened? He's out of his head. Will he die?"

Jacob could give no assurances. "Not if I can help it."

Margie bent her face to within a few inches of Thad's. "You ain't a gonna die if I got anything to say about it. You hear? Now get better." She resumed sponging him.

Teena lifted the poultice. "I see no change."

"Give it time." He'd used everything he knew. "It is in God's hands."

"Then you better start praying," Margie said. "Or send for Thomas."

"We can all pray," Teena said, stepping back from

the bedside. She lowered her head. Her eyes closed. Her lips moved silently.

Margie put down her damp cloth and moved to Teena's side. She, too, bowed her head and prayed silently.

Jacob hesitated. Perhaps he had no right to ask God to intervene. Wasn't it his fault the man had gotten so sick? He should have been here keeping watch, instead of wandering the streets, dreaming about a pleasant afternoon spent in Teena's company. In fact, if he had stayed here yesterday, perhaps he would have seen this coming.

He felt Teena's gaze on him. There was no accusation in her eyes, only a quiet waiting. He nodded, moved to her side and silently prayed. *God, I don't know that I deserve anything. Certainly my life is far from perfect. I confess I have entertained thoughts about Teena that would likely send her fleeing into the woods if she knew. However, I have tried to do my duty. Always. I have done all I can to help this man. I ask You to intervene and heal this grievous wound.*

The women returned to their tasks. Teena looked peaceful as if she expected God to answer her appeal.

Margie looked determined. She intended to fight for the life of this man.

Jacob did not know what he felt, other than uncertainty and a faint sense of guilt when his gaze lingered on Teena's face longer than it should, and he pulled his attention back to his patient.

* * *

Several hours later, Thad had not improved and Jacob feared the worst when he removed the poultice. The redness had grown wider.

Teena stepped back and clasped her hands together. "Jacob, I know you don't want any Tlingit ways in the clinic. I have always honored your scientific ways, wanting to learn your methods, but I know something that might fix this." She indicated the festering wound. "Will you give me permission to use it?"

He hesitated. Yes, many of her remedies were herbal, natural. But untested in a hospital situation. If he lost this patient because her methods poisoned him...

Sorrow and regret intertwined with fear. How would he explain another death at the hands of a native? To himself, let alone anyone else?

Margie made a loud noise—protest or exasperation—he couldn't say which. "Doc, think about the people she's helped. If this will save Thad, then let her do it."

Of course. He was again confusing Teena with the shaman who had treated Aaron. The two were miles apart in their methods. "Give it a try."

She retrieved her bag from the corner. Within minutes she had concocted a paste of several different powders and leaves. And she didn't once chant over the preparation.

He knew his silent comment was unfair, his anger misdirected at the one responsible for Aaron's death.

She removed his poultice, and pressed the paste to the wound, covering it with some sort of moss before she pulled the covers back over his leg. "I will make a tea." She hurried outside to heat the water.

Jacob stared after her.

"It's okay, Doc. She knows what she's doing."

The tea she returned with looked like boiled swamp water. She handed it to Margie. "See if he can drink, but don't let him choke."

Margie held the cup to Thad's lips and begged him to drink. Between threatening and cajoling, he emptied the pot.

Teena stepped back. "Now we wait."

Jacob and Teena sat on the edge of the second bed, facing the man, watching and waiting. Margie continued to sponge him, alternately threatening and begging him to get better.

Burns skidded into the room. "I wondered where you all were. Thought I might find supper." He sounded hopeful. Jacob often cooked an evening meal on the little stove.

"Thad is sick. We don't want to leave him." Jacob didn't have to ask either of the women to know they shared his opinion. "Run down the street and get us each a plate of food."

Burns dashed off to do as Jacob asked and returned half an hour later with plates piled high.

Margie shook her head when Jacob offered one to her. "I can't think about food when he looks like this."

"You need to keep your strength up."

She snorted. "Do I look like I'd fade away if I missed a meal or two?"

"You need to eat."

"Suppose you're gonna nag if I don't?"

He grinned.

With a mutter of resignation, she took the plate and scooped up huge forkfuls of food, finishing before either he or Teena were half-done.

She wiped her mouth. "You satisfied?" Without giving him a chance to answer, she returned to Thad's side and resumed washing him tenderly. Her actions were a contrast to the harsh words she rained over him.

The evening slipped by and the reluctant summer night descended, with no change in the man. But at least he wasn't worse.

"There's no point all of us staying," Jacob said. "Go home. Both of you. I'll remain with him." He lit a lantern.

Margie shook her head. "I ain't leaving."

"I'll stay," Teena said.

"Fine." Jacob grabbed a chair and got comfortable.

Margie pulled up a stool close to Thad's head and held his hand. Sometimes he slept. Sometimes he had his eyes open, rambling. When he woke, Margie spoke to him. "You gotta get better. You hear? I ain't letting you go."

Teena moved to Jacob's side. "Will you read from the Holy Word?"

The request was odd, given the circumstances, and yet perhaps not so odd. There was a quiet waiting in the atmosphere. He let the chair drop to all fours. Teena had already retrieved his bag and handed it to him. He pulled out his Bible. "Anything special you'd like me to read?"

"All of it." She grinned, her eyes catching the light from the lantern and throwing it back in a gleam.

She was teasing. He liked it. Liked the way their eyes held steadily, as if locked in an unending embrace. The way his heart thudded against his ribs was not so much exciting as enduring. The tip of each finger felt her as plainly as if they caressed her flawless skin.

"A Psalm would be good," Margie said, unmindful that her words had shattered a fragile moment.

Jacob pulled himself back to center and opened his little Bible, tipping it toward the light so he could see better.

Slowly, the words round and sweet on his tongue, he read. Teena sat on the floor at his feet. Again she watched his mouth, as if seeing the words with her eyes as well as hearing them with her ears. He didn't have to touch her to feel as if they shared an uncommon oneness. The words served to weave their hearts together.

His voice grew hoarse and he had to stop. Margie seemed to have fallen asleep with her head resting on the bed next to Thad's.

Teena rose in the graceful fluid way he had come to expect and enjoy. "I will check his wound." She hesitated. "Unless you…"

"Go ahead." He lifted the lantern above them so they could see.

Teena uncovered the area and sighed. "It is getting better."

"So I see." The redness had shrunk perceptively. "Let's see if the pus has cleared."

She shook her head. "Better to leave it."

Margie stirred, realized she had fallen asleep and bolted upright in her chair. "He's not—?" She swallowed loudly.

"He's resting."

She sank back, her hands pressed to her chest. "I dreamed…" She shook her head. "Don't matter what I dreamed. He's not dead."

Morning light flooded through the windows. Jacob pushed to his weary feet and stretched. Teena smiled, her eyes as bright as ever. Her braids neat, as if freshly done. He rubbed his chin, feeling old and rumpled.

"Hi. What's everyone doing here?"

Jacob jerked his gaze from Teena to Thad. The man's eyes were clear. His skin had a normal color.

Margie threw herself to his chest, loud sobs rending the air.

He patted her head and made shushing noises.

Finally she calmed, but kept her face pressed to his shirt. "I thought you were going to die."

He chuckled. "I didn't dare. Every time I opened my eyes you were there demanding I get better. I seem to recall a few dire threats."

Margie sat back on the chair, suddenly interested in a broken thumbnail.

Thad reached out and grabbed her hand. "Margie,

you were all I saw. All I cared about. Look at me." He waited for her to lift her face toward him. "When I get better will you marry me?"

She jerked her hands free. "You're mocking me."

"No, Margie. Never. I have grown to love you like I never dreamed was possible." His expression hardened and he turned to consider the ceiling. "Course, I understand if you refuse me. I might end up a cripple."

She bolted to her feet and glowered at him. "You think I would care about that? Then you don't know me."

He smiled. "I know you. Just as you know me. Promise to marry me when I'm better?"

"Pshaw. Of course I'll marry you." She bent, remembered Teena and Jacob. Never once shifting her gaze from Thad, she murmured, "A little privacy here."

Jacob laughed and reached for Teena. "We'll be outside if you need us."

"Think we can manage this on our own," Thad said, his voice thick.

"Crazy white man," Teena murmured, but her eyes sparkled and she smiled.

Jacob stared toward the trail. The morning was half-gone and Teena had not come. No need to worry, he assured himself. Perhaps she'd gone gathering berries and plants. She might have other things to attend to. Or…he had difficulty swallowing…she might be hurt.

Margie steadily refused to leave Thad's side. "I don't want him to change his mind about marrying me."

Jacob told her he was going to see what happened to delay Teena.

"Can't get along without her?" He ignored her mocking hoot of laughter. As he neared the village, he slowed his steps. Teena's father would not welcome his intrusion, but he must satisfy this restless uncertainty. He'd leave as soon as he knew Teena was okay.

He stepped into the opening. An elderly woman spotted him and shook her fists. He didn't need to know their language to understand what she meant.

Three more women hurried toward him, angry and loud.

"Teena," he called. "Where's Teena?" All he got was more shouting, more angry words. Where was Teena? He took a step forward. "I'm not leaving until I see Teena and make sure she's okay."

Teena heard him. The tension holding her in a clenched fist released, and she filled her lungs to the top for the first time since she'd realized her auntie was sick. It was a white man's illness. Jacob would know how to cure it. "Auntie, he will help us."

Auntie groaned as her bowels spasmed again. "I will die."

"No. You can't." Outside, some of the women were shouting insults at Jacob. Vile accusations, blaming him for killing them. He might not understand the words, but no one could mistake the venom behind them. She hurried outside.

Two aunties and a cousin blocked her path. "Haven't

we suffered enough because of the white man? He isn't welcome here."

"He can help."

The eldest woman stuck her face within an inch of Teena's. "You are responsible for this illness. We warned you to stay away from the white man's village. Now you have brought us another of their diseases."

Teena drew back, her heart accusing as much as the women's words. Her initial goal had been to learn the white man's healing ways. How long since she'd thought of that? Instead, she hurried down the trail every morning—not anxious to learn, but only eager to see Jacob. Why had she let herself be distracted? Why did she allow herself to believe impossible things about herself and Jacob? She regretted every wasted moment of dreaming, every misdirected thought. But right now she needed help. They all needed help. "He is our only chance to save our clan." She pushed past them, ignoring their threats and anger. "Jacob, I need you."

The look passing between them far exceeded a medical need. She swallowed back the rush of longing.

"My people are sick." She described the watery diarrhea, the sudden onset from first signs of illness to distress.

He made an explosive sound. "I feared this. I warned Mack we were ripe for an epidemic. How many are ill?"

"It started with my eldest auntie, but every time I look up it seems another person is grabbing at his belly."

"Where do you get your water?"

"Water is everywhere. The ocean. The rain. The river." She did not understand what he meant.

"What water do you drink?"

"From the river."

"That is likely the source of your problem. We have to act quickly. Will they let me see the sick ones?" He tipped his head toward the cluster of angry women.

She gave her relatives a hard look. "Follow me." She led him past the knot of threats, toward the lodge and inside.

The women followed, protesting loudly.

Teena stood in the middle of the building, turned full circle to engage all the occupants then spoke in her own language. "We are sick with a white man's disease. We all know how useless our ways are to treat it. This is Dr. Jacob, a white healer. He will know how to treat this illness."

A rumble of protests filled the room.

"We don't want help from his sort."

"He only brings more hardship."

"You are blinded by your heart."

She heard the last from a woman who had married Teena's cousin. She ignored it. Hoped no one else caught the words and misinterpreted them. Yes, her heart was involved, but she would not let it blind her to the facts. Neither should they.

Her father held up his hand, signaling for silence so he could speak. Slowly, the others quieted and waited for his decision. "You know my daughter is a wise healer. She learned it from her mother and her grandmother."

A murmur of agreement.

"She has told me of the things she has learned by helping this man." He paused to catch his breath. "We have lost many to their diseases. Will we lose more, rather than accept help from one of them?"

One by one the murmur of acceptance circled the room.

"Bring him in," Teena's father said. "Let him help us."

"Thank you, Father." She signaled for Jacob to come forward and led him to her auntie.

"When did she first become ill?"

"At first light she cried out with pain and rushed outdoors."

"How often have her bowels emptied?"

"Many times."

"Ask her if I can touch her. I want to see if she has a fever and check for dehydration."

Teena spoke to her auntie, who barely had the strength to nod.

His examination complete, Jacob turned to Teena. "It's cholera. It can take a person down in a matter of hours. The first thing is to rehydrate every sick person. I can make up a solution with basic things I have at the clinic—sugar, salt and baking soda. We'll need lots of water. Everything your people drink must be boiled. Tell them that."

He waited while she told the others.

"This place will have to be quarantined." He explained it meant no one could come in or go out. "This is so important that I need someone to enforce it."

"Jimmy is down on the beach. He'll do it if someone lets him know."

He went on to explain what other precautions were necessary. "You start boiling water, and lots of it, while I run back to the clinic and take care of the rest of it."

She turned to her cousin's wife. "Will you help me?"

The woman's face darkened. "You are not one of us any longer." She backed away and refused to help.

Teena looked about. "Will no one help? We cannot afford stubborn pride at the cost of our auntie, or..." She shifted her gaze to the child who moaned in the corner. "Or our children."

Only Auntie Lin, a woman who had lost her husband to an earlier epidemic of the pox, stepped forward. "I would have welcomed the chance to do something to save my husband. I will help you."

They filled pots with water and set them to boil. "I will watch the water," Auntie Lin said. "You take care of the sick."

Teena rushed from one sick person to another. Her old auntie had grown so weak, she wondered if it was too late for her.

Jacob ducked inside. "I'm back. Come and I'll show you how to mix up the solution."

She raced after him and listened carefully as he explained the amount of ingredients to put in each pot.

"Cool it enough to be comfortable, and get the sick drinking it."

"Is Jimmy coming?"

"He's on his way."

"What will he do?"

"Make sure no one comes or goes. The only way to keep this under control is to stop people from spreading it." He paused. "And hopefully find the source, though there's a good chance a carrier has moved on up the mountain. I've instructed Mack to inform the Mounties. So far, no one is sick in Treasure Creek, and I'd like to keep it that way."

"So why are my people sick? Is this punishment from God for something we aren't even aware of?" She understood God was loving. But also a righteous judge.

"You can't blame God for what men do to themselves."

"Someone did this to us? Do people hate us that much?"

"It isn't deliberate. People are careless with disposal of their waste. Right now they are in such a frantic hurry to get to the gold fields they forget common sense."

"White men are crazy." She felt no amusement in her announcement.

Jimmy reached the village and squatted at the trail. No one would get by him. But why were they forced to be prisoners because of something someone else had done? "Why doesn't God stop all this madness?"

"Is God responsible for what man chooses to do? Especially if they ignore His rules."

She didn't bother answering. She was much too busy running from one person to the next, as the disease spread from one to another. The women who had complained about Jacob fell ill and didn't protest when he came to their aid.

She lost track of time, only realizing the day had passed when dusk fell about them. Her old auntie grew weaker. She pulled Jacob aside. "She isn't getting better."

He shook his head. "Keep giving her the solution."

But a little later her auntie no longer responded, no longer swallowed when Teena held the cup to her mouth. Teena sat back on her heels, silencing the sorrow that ached at her lips. Now was not the time to give in to grief. Others were ill and still more falling ill. She returned to her auntie's side a short time later, knowing the end was near. When the last shuddering breath lifted her chest, Teena called Jacob. "She is gone."

"I'm sorry. I'll tell Jimmy. He knows what to do."

She wouldn't ask what would happen to Auntie's body. Now was not the time to worry about their usual customs. Now was the time to worry about the living, not the dead.

She moved among the sick. A couple of the earlier victims were resting more comfortably. Was the worst over? She prayed it was. She prayed God would show her people mercy.

"Jacob?" A voice called from outside.

"It's Mack. I asked him to check on us in the morning."

Teena struggled to lift her head, struggled to believe it was morning. She followed Jacob outside.

"Anyone sick in town?" he asked.

"No one so far."

"Did you post the warnings about boiling drinking water and—"

"There will be stiff fines for anyone not using proper latrines."

"Good. Almost everyone here has come down with it, but I'm hoping the worst is over."

"You both look tired. Can I send in someone to help?"

Jacob started to say no, then turned to consider Teena. "I'm sorry. I've been thinking of you as part of me." He shook his head. "I mean, as another pair of hands. Do you need help? Maybe Margie could come."

"I'm fine. Besides, who else can speak our language?" He thought of her as part of him? An equal? A unity? The idea renewed her strength and she returned to caring for the sick with all weariness gone.

A few days later it seemed the worst had passed. There'd been no one to fall ill for an hour or more. Those who were sick did not grow as weak as Auntie had. She and Jacob sat side-by-side outside, leaning against the lodge, able to rest for the first time in so long, she'd lost track.

She tipped her head against the wall, almost too tired to speak. But her heart was too full to remain silent. "I thank you for helping. You could have walked away."

* * *

Jacob was weary clear through. Moving required almost more effort than he could dredge up, but he slowly faced her. "Do you really think I could see you fighting to keep your family alive and not help?"

Her gaze sought something beyond his words. He let her search his soul. Let her see it was more than medical concern keeping him at her side throughout the long days and nights. He knew the moment she found his secret. Her eyes widened as if trying to drink it in. Her mouth curved in a pleased smile and then she ducked her head.

Dare he believe she didn't find his regard for her unwelcome?

"I would not have known what to do without your help."

"I will help you. You will help me." He repeated the words she had spoken at one of their earliest meetings.

Slowly, her head came up and she smiled at him. "I said that, didn't I?"

"I didn't believe you, but now I know it's true."

The look of regret in her eyes edged his thoughts with caution. Had he read more into the situation than he should? Certainly more than he had a right to.

He tried to think of all the reasons this could not be so. But none of them were strong enough to count.

"I am Tlingit." As if that encapsulated every possible objection.

"Would a Tlingit—" He had no right to ask if they

ever married a white. He shifted his thoughts. "What does being Tlingit mean?"

Pride filled her eyes. "Many things. It means family. Working together. Honor and honesty. It means tradition. Passing on clan secrets. Learning how to weave the secret patterns of our clan into a ceremonial robe." She grew curious. "What does being white mean?"

"There are many families, many clans in the white man's world. So, different things are important to different people."

"What is important to you?"

The question asked far more than the words. She again sought access to his heart and soul. Gladly, he would give it. "Family." He stopped. "My family is gone."

"I'm sorry." She squeezed his hand, sending a mixture of comfort and excitement through his nerves. "What happened?"

"My father died in an accident when I was a young man."

She ducked her head, hiding her face. "Are you not still a young man?"

"Compared to you I am ancient."

She gave him a hard look. "My auntie was ancient. You are not."

Oh, but she made him feel young again. Young and hopeful and…

"What happened to your mother? Was she in the same accident?"

He couldn't answer without talking about his brother.

Until this moment, he had not wanted to—but now he did. He wanted to share his sorrow and pain. Wanted her to comfort him. "My brother Aaron came north to search for gold. He was reckless, adventuresome. He got sick somewhere up here. An Indian shaman gave him something poisonous and it killed him. He's buried behind the church. My mother died of a broken heart." It was out. All out, and he drew in a breath that cleansed him.

"An Indian shaman? You are very sure?"

"I got a letter from the man Aaron traveled with. He didn't leave much doubt."

"I am very sorry, though I know of no shaman who would give poison."

"I expect it was not a person you know."

"Where is the rest of your family—aunts, uncles, cousins?"

He chuckled. "I am not as fortunate as you. My life is not blessed with many people. I am alone." He realized just how lonely he was, and reached for her hand.

She shied away.

Aware several people watched them, he lowered his hand, as if he meant all along to scratch his ankle.

"Daughter," Teena's father called.

She rushed to his side. Jacob followed.

"I fear I am sick."

Teena sent Jacob a desperate look, silently begging him to help. All he could do was assist the old man outside to empty his bowels, then help him back to his pallet. "Teena, give him lots of the fluid."

* * *

The next few hours were busy with alternately help-ing the old man outdoors and plying him with the solu-tion.

Teena pulled Jacob aside. "He will be all right, won't he?"

"We caught it early, and that seems to be the key."

"But he is so weak."

"Yes, he is weak."

"Dare I pray for him?"

He suspected she asked the question of herself, but he answered anyway, wanting to give her hope and encouragement. "Teena, we ask, and we trust God to answer as He sees fit. It isn't always how we want Him to answer."

"Then why ask?"

He knew the pat answers. *We have not because we ask not. Whatsoever ye shall ask for in prayer, believ-ing, ye shall receive.* But his prayers had not always been granted. Obviously, he did not have enough faith. How could he offer her comfort, when he didn't know the answers? He must try. "I suppose it's because God is our Heavenly Father." He spoke slowly, letting the ideas and words form at the same time. "Would your father give you something that would harm you?"

"Never."

"Would he ask you to do something difficult?"

She smiled. "Many times he has."

"Could it be the same with God?"

She studied him, taking from him a strength and

faith he didn't know he had. Satisfied, she nodded. "He loves us. That's what we have to believe."

Of course. It wasn't how much faith he had or how well he performed that mattered. It was how much God loved him. "Teena, I could hug you for making me see the wonderful truth about God's love."

Her face glowed, and then she looked frightened and backed away.

"I only meant it's made me very happy to realize this truth."

Chapter Eleven

God loved her. She would ask God to heal her father, trusting Him to answer out of love, not judgment. She silently made her request.

Father had been resting but now stirred. She rushed to his side.

"Daughter."

She bent close to hear his weak voice.

"I see you with this man." His eyes indicated Jacob standing behind her. "You feel something for him."

Teena hung her head but could not bring herself to deny it—yet, she was meant to marry a Wolf man…a man who stirred none of the joyful confusion in her heart that Jacob did. "I would never dishonor you by disobeying you."

He patted her hand. "I know. I know."

She wrapped her hands over his frail ones. They had once been so strong, holding her up when she took faltering steps, pulling her up a trail too difficult for her, gently teaching her, guiding her. When had he gotten so old and shrunken?

"What you feel for this man is in here." He pressed his hand to his chest. "In your heart."

She made a protesting noise. Not for anything did she want her father to be disappointed with her, or put him under the stress of insisting she follow his decision.

"Do not deny it. You must always honor the truth."

"Yes, Father. But I am Tlingit."

"This is the way it is meant to be. We must change or die. You will be the…" His voice faded. He struggled to keep his mind clear, and after a moment placed his fists together, then made a motion separating them by six inches, then drew them back together. "That will be your task."

"What task, Father? What do you mean?" But he had sunk into exhaustion.

He roused himself. "Call Auntie Lin over here."

She did so.

Her father waited until Auntie bent to his side, then his eyes brightened and he spoke clearly to Teena, raising his hand as if in blessing. "I release you from my promise to the man from the Wolf clan. You are free to follow your heart." He sought Auntie's acknowledging nod, then sank back, wearied by his efforts.

"But Father, what task is mine? Tell me."

He didn't answer. Didn't indicate he'd heard. She shook him. Limp. Turned to Jacob. "Do something. Don't let him die."

He touched his fingertips to her father's neck. His healing hands would bring her father back. They had to.

But Jacob only shook his head. "I'm sorry, Teena. He's gone."

She sank back on her heels. He couldn't be gone. She needed him. Needed him to explain what he meant. Sorrow swept up her like a raging floodwater, about to overwhelm her. She couldn't let Jacob see how much this hurt. Wouldn't reveal weakness to him.

He reached for her, as if to comfort her, but if she started to cry in front of him she would never be able to stop.

"Go." The word was harsh with a thousand unshed tears, a vast ocean of pain.

"Teena."

His concern threatened her sanity. She held up a hand to stop him from touching her. "Just go. Leave us alone."

He pushed to his feet but didn't move toward the doorway. He waited, silently begging her to reconsider.

She could not.

"You know where to find me when you're ready."

She listened to him leave the lodge. Gave him time to make it into the trees. Allowed five more gasps for him to get out of earshot, then she bent over her father's body and wailed.

Jacob knelt at Aaron's grave marker. Conflicting emotions raged through him. Gratitude that he had not shown any signs of cholera. Sorrow at Teena's loss. His own loss. Regret she had sent him away. Oh, how that hurt! Clear to the depths of his being, searing spots he didn't know, until now, even existed. Was she okay? A whiff of worry eased upward. It had been five days since he'd last seen her. Mack had checked on the village and said all the survivors were on the mend. He ached to go to her and comfort her, as she had comforted him— though she probably didn't know how much—with her explanation of God's love.

It was how much God loved *him* that mattered.

He did not have to prove himself worthy to God. The realization had loosened feelings of failure and disappointment in him, freeing him like a bird sent to wing.

Oh, Teena, where are you? Do you feel my heart calling to you?

He loved her. He knew it in his heart. He pressed his palm to his chest, as if to keep the precious feeling there.

Teena's father had made a similar gesture. He didn't know what the man had said, but at the way he glanced at Jacob, he wondered if it had something to do with him. He wished he could ask Teena.

Would she come back? He prayed she would.

Weeks later, Teena trudged the path leading to town. She'd tried to stay away. But her heart called her toward Jacob. He didn't know her father had said her heart now belonged to Jacob. For that she was grateful. But it didn't change things. No matter what Father said, nor if he blessed her feelings for Jacob, she was Tlingit. He was white. Those things could never change.

Jacob had said something. It teased the edges of thoughts. Suddenly, she recalled his words. They'd been talking about family. She'd said she was Tlingit. She meant it as a warning. He'd stopped before he voiced the question. But—she tried to tell herself she was only wishing, dreaming…had he been about to ask if a Tlingit would marry a white man? She let the joy of the thought sing through her heart, then forced it back. He had given her no reason to think he might ask. She was only letting her father's observations influence her. He was an old man. A wise old man who saw the yearning of Teena's heart. He did not see Jacob's heart.

She entered the building silently. Jacob had his back to her and stiffened, turning slowly to face her. He had known she was there, even though she had not made a sound. An eager, welcoming light filled his eyes.

He didn't speak, just looked at her.

Sunlight filled the room. Love—undeniable, unstoppable, pure and sweet—flooded her heart, overflowed until she felt as if she stood in a great pool of sweet, warm love. She could drown in it. Gladly. Eagerly.

But why did he look so stunned? Had her feelings spoken to him? She blinked, lowered her gaze, but could not keep it away from him.

"Teena." Her name barely made a sound. He stepped toward her. "I didn't know if you'd come back. You were so angry."

"I wasn't angry." He'd missed her. It was as plain as the dust motes floating in the overbright light. "You mistook my sorrow for anger."

He nodded. "I'm glad." Then he swiped a hand across his face as if he could erase the words. "I'm glad you're here." He closed the distance between them until they stood close enough to touch, but neither of them made an effort to do so.

Teena didn't need to feel him with her fingers, she felt him in every pore of her skin, every beat of her heart, every sweet, warm breath that filled her lungs.

"Are you okay?"

"I'm fine." Sorrow had become a familiar shawl. Not one she welcomed, but one she wore with as much dignity as she could muster.

"How are your people?"

"No one else has died, and people are getting their strength back." There was one exception. "One old auntie remains weak, complaining she is useless and should be left to die. I tell her we need her. Who would teach the young people the traditions and stories of the Tlingit if all the old people die?"

"Do you want me to look at her?"

Did she want him back at the village where memories of him clung to every corner? "I will ask her if she will allow it." But she doubted he would be welcome back in the village. The majority of them blamed him simply because he was white, overlooking that he had helped many survive.

He nodded, his gaze holding her in an unbroken grasp.

She recalled the feeling she'd had on the mountain when rescuing Martin—as if a rope secured their hearts together. She felt something stronger, more enduring connecting their gazes.

"I'm glad you're here." He brushed his hand to her head.

Never had she known such sweet communion with another human—white or native. And she let her eyes say all her heart felt.

His gaze answered in kind.

Joy sweetened her insides.

"Well, lookee who's back?"

At Margie's loud voice behind her, Teena and Jacob each stepped back, the moment gone, but the feeling forever in her heart.

"Glad to see you back. Sorry about your father."

"Thank you." She pulled her thoughts firmly back to the here and now. "How is Thad?"

"See for yourself." Margie waved her into the next room. Thad grinned from his bed.

"Heard my Margie coming. Thought you'd never get here, girl. Thought maybe you'd changed your mind about an old cripple and I was going to have to die of lonesomeness."

Margie laughed uproariously. "'Twould take a team of oxen and a dozen strong men to keep me away, and I ain't never gonna change my mind."

Thad's grin went from ear to ear. A very pleased man.

"Teena, have a look at his leg." Jacob lifted the blanket for her to see. "It's clean and healed. Thanks to you."

At the tremor in his voice that likely no one else heard, she could not look at him, fearing it would be her undoing. Instead, she examined the wound as if it needed far more attention than it did. Finally she straightened. "It looks fine."

Jacob chuckled softly. "Everything is fine indeed."

She could close her eyes and drift on his approval, even though she understood he meant more than Thad's wound—though they all found that good news.

Someone outside the clinic called for the doctor. Jacob sighed. "Time to get to work. Teena, are you coming?" He waited for her to join him.

It felt right and good to be back at his side.

They saw a dozen men with injuries requiring stitches. Half a dozen more with various minor complaints.

"No one in Treasure Creek got the cholera?"

"I'm very relieved the epidemic was contained, though I regret it was your village it hit."

"Me, too. But you taught me how to treat it. Because of you, we didn't lose near as many as we could have."

"I help you. You help me. Remember?"

"How do I help you?"

"Besides Thad? I can't begin to tell you."

She wasn't sure what he meant, and feared to ask him, lest his answer didn't satisfy the hungry longing of her heart.

Jacob welcomed her back. She was as capable as ever. She seemed glad to be helping again. The first day, he was certain an eager light filled her eyes. As happy to see him as he was to see her. He saw the flash in her eyes often, and he allowed himself to hope she might see him as more than a white doctor to teach her white man's ways. He wanted her to see him as a man.

But so often she pulled back into herself, as if shying away from him. Did she blame him in some small way for her father's death? There'd been nothing he could do to save the old man. He was too weak, too emaciated. But did it look to Teena like he hadn't tried?

He wanted to say something, tell her how he felt, but he recognized her need to mourn.

But as each day passed, his heart grew more impatient, as if it could not continue to hold back his feelings without doing irreparable damage. Waiting made him edgy, at times irritable.

This could not go on.

They had not been up the Chilkoot Trail since the cholera epidemic. Seems everyone realized they could find medical help in Treasure Creek, and came with their injuries or injured.

The last time they'd been up there had been special to Jacob—he hoped to Teena, as well. He looked about. No one waited to see him. No one called from the beach.

Margie kept Thad company as she did as many hours a day she could manage. In fact, she'd left Frankie to finish the work at the church tower on her own...with Lucy's erratic help.

Burns had dashed in a few minutes ago with the announcement he and the dog, Yukon, were going exploring.

Nothing kept Jacob at the clinic, and much called to him from the mountain.

"Teena, come with me to check the trail." He grabbed his bag.

She slung her pack over her shoulder, an eager glow in her eyes.

He liked the trail close to town, passing as it did through the rain forest. The air was moist and musky. People less frantic than they were past Sheep Camp, and facing the steep ascent to the top. With no agenda in mind except spending time in Teena's company, he kept a leisurely pace, pausing often to ask her about the vegetation at the side of the trail. "What plant did you give Donald that made him happy?" He'd often wondered what she'd given his earliest patient.

She stepped from the path and indicated he should follow her. They entered a boggy area and she looked about. "There." She indicated a cluster of flowers. "Allheal. In summer, the entire plant is useful. But the fall root is the most powerful." She plucked a plant and handed it to him.

He sniffed it and examined it, then tucked it in his

bag. He would see what he could find in his reference books.

Rather than return to the trail, they found a dry spot and sat. He asked her what the natives did during the long winter night.

"We weave and carve."

He pressed for more information, wanting to see Teena more clearly.

"We make baskets from spruce root, robes from mountain goat wool and cedar bark strips."

"It sounds…" He searched for a word to express how comforting it seemed in his imagination—family all gathered together working inside, warm and dry. "… like one great, big, happy family."

"We are. Of course we argue and disagree, but only in fun for the most part. Harmony is important when living in such close quarters, so when the eldest auntie declares it's time to stop discussing something that has grown heated, we all obey. It is the honor of a Tlingit to obey."

He tried to paint a picture of life in Seattle, with people hurrying about, the edge of competitiveness he'd never paid attention to before now. "But I guess you've seen how it is with all these people heading for the gold fields."

"White men are crazy." She grinned.

He loved it when she teased. "I expect even the natives have some odd habits."

She pretended great shock. "I know of none."

He laughed and the tension of the last few days escaped. "This is really a beautiful country."

She rolled her eyes. "It was."

"Before the gold rush stampede."

"Before the crazy white man came."

"But we aren't the first."

She chuckled. "But probably the worst."

He knew she teased, but the element of truth was inescapable. "I guess you get to see the worst."

Her gaze darkened, grew direct, sank deep into his thoughts. "And also the best."

Pleased beyond description at her assessment, knowing she meant him, he grinned. It seemed the right atmosphere to tell her how he felt about her. "Teena?"

She'd shifted her gaze. "Would you mind reading the Holy Word?"

He pulled his thoughts back from the trail they headed down. "I will do better. I will teach you to read."

Her face rounded with awe. "You will? Now?"

He chuckled. "I think it will take a bit longer than that. I'll start tonight, if you like."

She nodded, her expression so eager he wondered if he should consider giving up doctoring to be her teacher. The idea gave him a great deal of pleasure.

"You'll read to me now, though?"

"Of course." At her request, he often read a chapter or two. He never offered to read on his own, although the thought came frequently. He preferred to have her ask, to feel she needed him, perhaps enjoyed the feeling of closeness it provided as much as he did.

"I will read to you from the Gospel of John." He explained who John was. "Jesus's beloved friend."

As always, she drank in the words from his mouth.

He read for an hour or more, until his voice grew hoarse. He closed his Bible and leaned toward her. "Teena, you and I have grown to be good friends. Is that not so?"

She nodded, her gaze open and welcoming.

He touched her head as he had only one time before. Her hair glistened in the sunlight, giving back the warmth of its rays. He lowered his hand, his fingers trailing down her cheek to her jaw.

Not once did she blink or withdraw either in her body or her eyes.

He ran his fingertip across her chin, pausing below her lips. "Teena, is it possible we have something more than friendship?"

Her mouth curved as if she had a secret.

He cupped her chin in his palm and studied her, taking in each detail—the golden flawlessness of her skin, the red of her lips, the black watchfulness of her eyes. "I want you to consider if it's possible for a beautiful Tlingit woman to marry an older, crazy white man."

Her gaze promised so much, but he wouldn't push her. He'd said enough for one day. He kissed her quickly, gently, a promise of his love and patience, then he drew back, his thumb pad lingering on her lips. "I only want you to think about it."

She lowered her gaze. "I will think about it."

It was enough. "I suppose we'd better return, in case I am needed." He reached for her hand and pulled her to her feet, kept holding her hand as they returned to the trail and headed toward town.

She thought about what he said as she walked the trail between her village and his. She thought of it when Viola called her in to visit, which she did often, since learning that Teena had discovered the truth about the woman claiming to be Goldie's aunt.

"I can't thank you enough," she said so many times that Teena had protested. But a friendship had grown between them. Viola treated her with the same acceptance Sarah had.

Teena paused out of sight of the cabin. She longed to tell Viola of her confusion, but whenever a man's name entered the conversation, Viola's eyes grew hard and wary. Teena recognized that a secret hurt drew Viola's heart tight, but she respected her friend too much to pry into the cause.

She thought about Jacob's words as she helped prepare meals and tend to her old auntie, and, as she lay on her pallet, she thought of them some more.

But she had no answers. Only questions.

She loved him. That was not something that needed considering. She pressed her hand to her chest, covering her heart. Even if she tried to pretend otherwise, her heart would always speak the truth.

But there were many other things to consider. Although her father had released her from his promise to marry her to a Wolf man, her clan would not understand her marrying a white. She did not want to be cut off from her family.

Even worse, would Jacob change his mind about her with the passing of time, perhaps decide to return to his old life in Seattle? Who would she be then?

She felt Jacob's quiet waiting the next day, but she was no closer to an answer—and he seemed prepared to let her take her time thinking about it.

They worked together in pleasant routine, but when he brushed his hand across hers in tending a patient, her insides went soft as spring snow, then just as quickly turned brittle as winter ice. Could a Tlingit love a white man? Could a white man love a Tlingit? Would both be rejected by their people?

He waited for the patient to leave, then indicated she should follow him outdoors, where Thad could not overhear them. "Teena, I've made you nervous and I'm sorry. Can you forget what I said?"

Her heart plummeted. Her gaze jerked to his. "You did not mean it?"

His smile filled his eyes with sadness. "I meant it. But I do not wish to upset you."

She looked deeply into his eyes. Into his heart. Saw that he cared. "I do not wish you to change your mind."

He caught her chin with the tip of his finger and studied her with such love her knees felt weak. "Are you saying you think there is a chance for us to…?" He left the question unfinished.

She closed her eyes. "I don't know. There is much to consider. I need time to think."

His finger lingered, exerting gentle pressure. "Look at me, Teena."

She did so willingly, needing to see his true feelings.

"I will give you all the time you need. You surely understand that."

She nodded.

"I pray you will find the answers you need and give me the answer I long for."

He smiled at her, filling her heart with liquid sunshine. He lowered his head. Did he mean to kiss her? She closed her eyes. Waited. Felt his breath across her cheeks.

"Doc. Teena." Lucy's loud voice caused them both to jerk away. "I've been looking for you. Thought I'd find you in the clinic, not out back here. Never mind. You are both invited to our house—Caleb's and mine—for supper tonight."

Jacob cleared his throat and seemed to struggle for words. "A special occasion?"

"Come along and see." Lucy winked at Teena. Teena knew the surprise Lucy had planned, but she wouldn't breathe a word of it ahead of time. "You coming or not?"

"I'll be there," Teena said.

"I will, too."

Lucy stomped off to invite the others on her list. She'd planned who she meant to come to this first dinner.

"That's odd," Jacob said.

"What? Being invited to share a meal?"

Jacob looked confused. "Is she a better cook than Margie?"

Teena chuckled. "Margie does her best." True, some of the meals were a little…well, hastily prepared. It didn't seem to matter to Margie if the food was all cooked at the same time, or if some got dry and chewy while other parts were wanting a little longer over the fire.

"I know she does." He sounded doubtful.

Teena could hardly wait for supper. Besides, the diversion gave her something to think about besides Jacob's question and her disappointment that Lucy had interrupted what Teena was certain would have been a kiss.

Later, she and Jacob walked together to Lucy and Caleb's cabin. For the few minutes it took to reach the place, Teena let herself think this would be how it felt if a Tlingit girl married a white man. Walking side by side toward a shared event. She allowed herself to enjoy the moment—Jacob at her side, touching her elbow to guide her past puddles in the street, standing back to let her go first when they reached the Johnson cabin and Caleb opened the door to them.

According to Lucy's plans, they arrived before her

sisters. Lana and Mack, with young Georgie, were already there, as were Hattie, Viola and baby Goldie. Hattie and Viola grinned widely, aware of the surprise.

Knowing how Lucy had worked so hard, with Viola's help, to make new curtains, a fancy tablecloth and other things she called improvements, Teena glanced about the room. The white, lace-edged curtains did look nice on the window. Dishes were set on the table, half hiding the crisp, white tablecloth. And the food smelled good. Lucy had promised cookies for later. Teena's mouth watered at the prospect.

Boots sounded outside and the gruff voices of Margie and Frankie were arguing about something.

Lucy sprang to the door. "I can hardly wait to see their reaction." She threw open the door. "Come on in." Stepping aside, she waved them into the big room. "What do you think?"

Frankie looked at Lucy. "Why you all dressed up?" She wore a simple dress she'd had Viola help her make.

Lucy's face colored up. "It's nothing fancy. That's not what I meant. Look at the curtains." She pointed out all the improvements. Margie seemed impressed. At least she gave them closer study. But Frankie tossed her hands upward. "You've gone all fancy, haven't you?"

Lucy smiled gently. "I've done my best to turn Caleb's place into a home."

Caleb moved to his wife's side. "And I appreciate it. I don't know how I'd have gotten through these past few weeks without your sweet comfort." He touched his chin to her head.

"No word?" Mack asked.

"Nothing. I know Leo did wrong." He turned to Lana. "He wasn't acting right when he took your gold pin, but he's never been strong here." He touched his head. "I thank God that you weren't seriously injured when he tried to find the gold, using Mack's mysterious map. But I miss the boy. I worry about him."

For a moment, no one spoke. Leo, a grown boy with a child's mind, had forced Lana to go with him, hoping to find Mack's hidden gold with the map Mack had given to Lana. Instead, he'd grown frustrated because he couldn't read the map, and had pushed Lana to the ground after nicking her with his knife. Rather than face Mack or his father, he'd run off and hadn't been heard from since, nor had anyone seen him.

Mack went to Caleb's side. "It was my own fault for thinking I could hide my gold. I learned my lesson. Now I have only land. No one can take it. No one can steal it. My family is safe. I'm sorry that Leo became a victim in all this."

Caleb grabbed Mack's hand. "He made his own choices. I would rest easier if I heard from him, though."

Teena met Jacob's glance, feeling the same sadness in him that poured through her. Greed for gold destroyed not only the land but people's lives.

She couldn't look away from his intensity. He hadn't spoken of them being together again, just as he promised, but she felt his silent question in his gaze, and gave a regretful shake of her head. She still did not have the answers she needed.

Caleb squeezed Lucy close. "Sorry for ruining your party by talking about sad things."

Lucy wrapped her arms about his waist and hugged him. "It's not ruined, and I think everyone understands how you worry about your son." She faced the others. "Now, let's eat." She indicated where each should sit.

Teena ended up at Jacob's side. The table was small enough that their elbows brushed each time they moved. Sweet misery for Teena. How could she think rationally, when this unavoidable touch reached into her heart and reminded her of how much she loved him?

She deliberately focused on Frankie and Margie as they tasted the food Lucy had prepared. This was the surprise Lucy had in mind…proving to her sisters that learning to be a housewife wasn't a waste of time.

Frankie held the roast venison in her mouth and moaned. "You never cooked like this before."

Lucy grinned at Hattie. "I've been taking lessons."

Margie stirred the gravy round and round, then gingerly tasted it. Her eyes widened. "You made this? By yourself?"

Lucy laughed. "I want to be a good wife. Figured that meant learning to make a decent meal." She waited as everyone tasted the food. "What do you think?"

"It's excellent," Lana said, and the others echoed their approval.

Frankie rested her fists beside her plate. "Might be

handy for one of us to know how to cook." Then she returned to her food.

Lucy grinned.

A little later, she served tea and a plate of cookies.

"Cookies?" Georgie said.

She handed him one.

He bit it. Saliva ran from the corners of his mouth and he sucked it back loudly. "Good cookie."

Frankie tasted one. "I suppose mine won't be good enough for the young gentleman now."

Lana chuckled softly. "Georgie likes cookies of all sorts, don't you, young man?"

His mouth too full for him to speak, he nodded.

But Frankie's glance at Lucy was full of curious caution, as if she wasn't certain what to make of the changes in her youngest sister.

Teena wished the evening could last forever. With all the conversation and joking around the table, she barely had time to consider her quandary. But she let her heart enjoy sharing each moment with Jacob. Later, Jacob walked with her through the tree-shadowed paths to the Tlingit village.

They paused as if by mutual agreement. He touched her shoulder, brushed his knuckles along her cheek. "Are you still thinking?"

She knew what he meant. "There is much to consider."

"We could be happy together."

She didn't answer. There were so many other things to consider besides their own happiness. It wasn't fair to keep him waiting, but until she knew the answers she could not tell him. She loved him. But was it really possible for them to be happy together? Their worlds were so different.

Every morning, as she trod the trail through the trees, she considered the questions. Today was no different.

So far, she had no answers.

She reached the edge of town and hesitated. She didn't want to face Jacob with her emotions so close to the surface. Instead of going to the clinic, she shifted direction and made her way along the side of town. At the cross street she turned right toward the church. The cemetery at the back was quiet and peaceful. No one would bother her there.

However, a figure knelt at a grave. A familiar figure. She blinked and stared. Jacob. She ground to a halt and slid into the shadows. She tried to think what grave was in that particular spot, but couldn't be certain. She watched him for a moment and was about to slip away, when he pushed to his feet and headed toward the clinic without so much as a sideways look.

She waited until he disappeared, then slipped toward the place where he had knelt. She knew this grave. Had found the man up the mountain. He had been very sick. His body full of infection. Beyond help. He died despite her best efforts. Jimmy had carried him down and Mack arranged a proper burial. She studied the letters on the cross. "C-A-L-L-O-W-A-Y." The same letters as on Jacob's sign. *Calloway.*

A shudder raced up her insides. This was Jacob's brother. He blamed a shaman for his death. Had accused that person of poisoning him. She was the Tlingit who had tried to save him. If he'd been poisoned, it wasn't at her hands. But Jacob thought otherwise.

She backed away from the grave until she reached the shelter of the church and sank to the ground in the shadow of the building.

Jacob made no secret of what he felt about the native who had treated his brother. If he knew it was her, he would hate her.

She wouldn't tell him. She'd pretend she didn't know. She'd hide the truth.

"You must always honor the truth." Her father's words echoed inside her.

"The Tlingit believe in honesty," she'd told Jacob, with more than a hint of pride.

But this was a unique situation. The truth would only hurt everyone. She pushed to her feet and resolutely headed for the clinic.

She was right not to tell him. It would only add to his pain at his brother's death.

Chapter Twelve

She hesitated before the clinic. How would she hide the awful way she felt, knowing he blamed her for his brother's death? It took every skill of self-control she knew to mask her face and deny her heart. Then she stepped inside.

Jacob sat behind the small desk in the room where he saw patients. He glanced up at her approach and smiled.

All her carefully schooled resistance fled and she faltered, considered backing out the door and fleeing to the mountains where he would not find her.

"Look what I found." He indicated a book.

Who would teach her to read, if he knew the truth?

"See. Your all-heal plant is also known as valeriana, a plant containing the alkaloids chatinin and valerine, which act as central nervous system depressants."

She studied the picture, saw the familiar flower.

"A native plant that calms fears, soothes a woman's monthly pain and makes anxious people happy."

"Is it better coming from a book?"

He closed the pages and pushed the thick book aside. "You trust what you've been taught by your mother and grandmother. I trust what I've been taught from older, wiser teachers, as well. Only, they talk to me from these books."

"You trust books more than people?"

"Sometimes. Not all books of course, but books like these are read and tested by many. Haven't you found that people don't always tell you the truth? Sometimes they don't even know it?"

"True." She wanted to say it was more so with the white man than the natives, but her heart kicked up such a protest she couldn't. She was hiding a guilty secret. If only she could believe he would understand.

Patients began arriving and she was grateful for the distraction. A man came in with splinters in his face. A box had been dropped, broken upon impact and sprayed the man. One splinter stuck into the man's eye. "Can you fix it?" she asked Jacob.

"I'll try." He had the man lie on the bed and instructed three men to help. "Hold him firm. I don't want him to move when I tackle his eye." As he eased the splinter loose, he explained what he was doing. Always, he taught Teena as he worked.

Who would teach her how to be a nurse, if he knew she was the one he held responsible for his brother's death?

He bandaged the man's eye and told him to come back in the morning so he could check it.

* * *

They were busy until late afternoon. Burns trotted by and Jacob called him. "Bring us a sandwich from the restaurant." He set the kettle to boil. "Let's have tea."

She hesitated. But if she refused he would wonder why. And her only excuse was her troubled conscience. So she joined him, lounging side by side against the shaded side of the building.

"Mack expects the church bell to arrive on the next boat from Seattle," he said.

"Hasn't he said that for the last three boats?" She glanced at him and they laughed.

"Mack is the eternal optimist."

"Margie said Frankie has almost finished the bell tower."

"Have you ever heard a big bell ringing?"

She shook her head.

"You'll like it."

"Okay." How could he be so certain?

"Do you suppose Lana will plan a party to celebrate the bell's arrival?"

She laughed. "Lana plans a big party for every occasion—great or small."

He chuckled.

Their eyes caught in shared amusement and so much more.

She jerked away. Who would be her friend if she told him the truth?

"Do you want another reading lesson?" he asked.

She already knew all the letters and could read a

few words. She hungered to read the books stacked on a shelf in the clinic, but she shook her head. "I must go back to my village."

"Oh. Tomorrow, then?"

His disappointment gathered in a knot inside her heart. He would be so hurt if he knew the truth. But she feared his anger more than anything. Only once had she seen him angry. It had been when a man and woman brought in their little son. He was so weak he could barely breathe. His chest was sunken, indicating he had been sick a long time.

"Why didn't you bring him sooner?" Jacob demanded.

"Didn't have time, Doc," the man mumbled.

"How could you not have time to look after your child? It will be a wonder if he survives." The look Jacob gave Teena said he knew the man was too busy looking for gold. Anger had flashed from his eyes.

Teena shuddered, grateful it wasn't directed at her.

Jacob fought for that little life for three days, without taking time to sleep. He only ate because Teena made sure food was placed in front of him.

The wee one recovered. When Jacob released him to his parents he had not spared them the blunt edge of his anger. "This child is more valuable than any amount of gold you find. If I learn he has died of neglect, I will see you are charged with that and anything else I can persuade the law to throw at you." He had been loud and direct, giving the pair nothing to misunderstand. "Do you hear me?"

He was a tall man, but it was the first time Teena had seen him use his size for intimidation.

The pair had mumbled agreement and slunk away.

Teena did not want to invite that sort of reaction from Jacob by telling him the truth about Aaron.

She longed to sit at his side, with him bent close, teaching her to read. Instead, she had to deny herself because her secret made it impossible to think clearly. "Maybe tomorrow," she agreed, almost changing her mind about leaving.

As she wandered down the trail toward the village, a question hounded her. What was she going to do?

She couldn't pray, because she knew God's answer. *Speak the truth.*

Even if her father were still alive she wouldn't ask him, knowing how highly he valued honesty.

Rather than return to the village, she shifted direction and headed for a quiet spot in the trees, where she sank to the ground and tried to think. But every thought she pursued returned to the same place—she was living a lie. She, who prided herself on being Tlingit, had resorted to hiding the truth.

The stillness wrapped about her, broken by nonintrusive sounds of birds and leaves. In the distance, the murmur of the river. She let the silence sift through her thoughts, let it sink into her heart. Faced the brutal truth. Her secret was destroying her soul, but she feared telling Jacob the truth.

* * *

She fought her battle all night. Morning came. She helped those weakened by cholera. Made sure they were comfortable. Ignored the hard looks her cousin's wife gave her, silently blaming her for the recent deaths. She faced accusations and blame from her own clan. That she could endure. But how would she survive if Jacob learned the truth about her part in his brother's death?

The truth shall make you free.

She pushed the words from her mind. Would not let herself remember how Mr. McIntyre had said them often, read them from God's word. Sometimes the truth could hurt.

The battle raged on as she made her way to the clinic. Part of her considered avoiding the place altogether, but another part—a stronger, more insistent part—would not let her stay away. She wanted to learn all she could from Jacob while she had the opportunity.

The truth was, she wanted to spend every minute available to her with him.

It was a truth she could not deny.

Jacob and Thad were visiting when she stepped into the room. Jacob smiled as she entered. "Thad's been telling me how he plans to settle here in Treasure Creek when he's up and about again."

"With Margie at my side." The man grinned from ear to ear. "I found a good woman when I met her."

Teena felt Jacob watching her. Knew he was silently asking if they could have what Thad and Margie had.

She couldn't meet his gaze. Couldn't let him see the uncertainty in her eyes, which he'd doubtless read as her decision that he was too old…that a Tlingit and a white could not share that kind of joy.

She loved him. That was not under question.

But would he love her once he learned the truth?

Several people came by for various minor complaints. Teena kept busy, though Jacob might have wondered why she so often paused to stare out across the water. Twice he'd given her a considering look and headed her direction.

She hurried back to her tasks before he could ask her what pulled her away from this place.

Thankfully, they were busy enough to keep her from brooding, but not so busy she didn't have time to wonder how she could continue to hide the truth. Then, suddenly, no one waited to be seen by the doctor. Margie quietly visited Thad at his bed. Jacob sat at the desk.

"Seems we're done for the day, barring any emergency. Would you like to—" His words were cut off by a knock on the door. A weary-looking man pushed his battered hat back on his head.

"I take it you're the doctor."

Teena had seen such weary men before, returning from a fruitless attempt to cross the mountains, beaten by the forces of nature. She wondered what he wanted from Jacob. The doctor did not have a remedy for defeat and discouragement. Best he find Mack or Thomas, and ask to hear God's word.

"I was to deliver this message to someone in this town. A person who would know what to do with it."

Jacob's eyebrows crooked. "That's rather vague."

"The Mounties said to give it to Mr. Tanner, or a preacher or doctor. I saw the sign 'Tanner's General Store' and stopped there, but the folks told me Mr. Tanner was unavailable. Said he was the only preacher you folks have, so that left the doctor. You." He dropped a sealed letter before Jacob. "I done what I was asked. The rest is up to you." He touched the brim of his hat in a goodbye gesture and hurried away.

Jacob and Teena both stared at the letter.

She edged closer. It felt sinister, threatening. She wanted to press to Jacob's side. Feel his arm about her. But she had no right, and she stiffened.

"Well, only one way to find out what this is all about." He picked it up. "It's addressed 'To Whom It May Concern.' I guess that's me." He broke the seal and pulled out a bit of paper. Read the contents aloud.

"This letter contains information regarding one Leo Johnson. Because of the nature of the news, I deemed it best to relay the facts to someone in authority who could see that his father is informed in a compassionate manner."

Jacob stopped reading and met Teena's gaze. "That sounds ominous." He ducked his head and continued.

"I am sad to inform you that Leo is dead. The facts of his demise are thus. He attached himself to a group of prospectors in the hopes of discovering gold. Upon learning that one of them had a fair-sized poke, young Leo tried to acquire treasure by lightening the poke. A altercation ensued, and in the fight, Leo was shot. May God have mercy on his soul. My condolences to his family.
Signed, Constable Anthony Jones, NWMP.

Teena gulped. "How dreadful."

"I have to tell Caleb." He pushed heavily to his feet. "Would you come with me?"

She nodded. "Poor Caleb."

He ducked around the door to tell Thad and Maggie they had an errand to attend to. Then he reached for Teena's elbow. Not that she needed help walking. Perhaps he found as much comfort in the contact as she. Perhaps she could count on that mutual awareness to hold them together if she confessed the truth.

But would it be enough?

Was she willing to take the risk?

He turned toward the church. "I think we should let Lucy know, so she can be with him." But only Frankie worked at the church. "Has Lucy gone home?"

Putting backs on the benches, Frankie battered at some boards before she answered. "Us Tuckers came here to start a new life. The three of us always made it on our own. But Lucy, and now Margie, changed their tunes." She glowered in the direction of Caleb's and Lucy's cabin. "That sister of mine spends more time catering to her husband than she does helping me." As if remembering Jacob had asked a question, she sighed and turned to them. "She left a bit ago. Got to make a fine supper for her man, she says."

"Thanks." Jacob waited until they had turned the corner, out of sight and hearing, to chuckle. "Seems Frankie thinks Lucy has settled for less than the best by getting married."

"And now Margie is going to marry Thad."

"Poor Frankie." But they glanced at each other and smiled.

His gaze caught and held hers, promising a future together that matched—surpassed—the happiness Lucy and Caleb had found.

A happiness that could be shattered by the truth. "It's a shame we have to take them such bad news."

Jacob nodded, his eyes sorrowful. "Sometimes the truth can't be avoided."

Sometimes it could. At least temporarily.

They arrived at the cabin. Hesitated. But Caleb had seen them and threw open the door. "Come on in. You're just in time for supper."

"We didn't come to interrupt your meal."

"You're more than welcome," Lucy said.

"I've brought news of Leo."

Teena heard the strain in Jacob's voice and wished she could offer him comfort. All she could do was smile encouragement.

Caleb's face flooded with joy. Then as quickly, guardedness replaced his look. "If it was good news you wouldn't be here."

Lucy rushed to his side.

"It is bad news."

"He's dead, isn't he?"

"I'm sorry." Jacob stilled.

Teena brushed his elbow in silent sympathy. He flicked a glance toward her, seemed to find the strength to continue.

"The details are in this letter."

Caleb did not raise a hand to take it. "Read it to me." His voice broke.

Jacob cleared his throat and read it aloud. A heavy silence filled the room when he finished. And then Caleb groaned.

Lucy wrapped her arms about him and held him tight.

"I'm sorry." Jacob gently placed the letter on the table and backed away.

Teena hesitated. "I, too, am sorry. Perhaps it would be better if you didn't know the truth." Surely there were times when not knowing was better.

Caleb lifted a misery-filled gaze to her. "It is better to know than to wonder. The truth frees me to move on."

Teena shuffled back. His words echoed the holy words Mr. McIntyre had taught her.

She could not keep her secret. Tomorrow she would

tell Jacob the truth. It meant facing Jacob's anger. Losing his friendship.

How would she survive without her teacher, her friend? The love in her heart would never die, but she knew it would also never know fulfillment.

The next morning, her resolve faltered as she approached the clinic. Would this be her last day there? Perhaps she should wait until afternoon to tell him.

But she could not. If she didn't tell him at once, it would only get more difficult.

She stepped inside. He sat at the desk, poring over one of his many books. She studied him hungrily. His dark brown hair so thick it made her want to slip her fingers into its depths. His square jaw signaling his uncompromising nature. She swallowed hard. That very trait she admired immensely would be what made him turn from her after he heard her confession. She completed her study of him. The cleft in his chin. How often had she wanted to touch that spot with the tip of her finger? Would she never get the chance?

He looked up, saw her and gave a smile full of warmth and welcome.

She faltered. Must she risk all this for the sake of truth?

She must. Both as a Christian and a Tlingit.

"I need to tell you something."

He waited. "Go ahead."

How? How could she tell him? The simple truth

seemed so naked and cruel. "Can we go for a little walk?"

He pushed to his feet. "Is there anyone waiting outside to see a doctor?"

"Not yet." It was now or never. "This won't take long."

"Then by all means, tell me what's so important."

They stepped outside and she indicated they should head toward the church. Neither of them spoke, the silence heavy with anticipation on his part and dread on hers.

They reached the church and her steps faltered.

"What is it?" He looked about, as if expecting something out of the ordinary.

"Not here." She continued to the cemetery. The truth was right before them, only, each had a differing version of it. She stopped in front of his brother's grave and read the name. "Calloway."

"It's my brother." His smiled was sad, with a hint of irony. "You can read that now."

She nodded. "You said a shaman killed him."

"Yes, poisoned."

"He was not poisoned. At least not by the native healer."

His eyes narrowed. "What makes you so certain?"

She wanted to grab his arm, make it impossible for him to escape without hearing the whole story—her side of it. "I tried to help him."

Horror filled his eyes. "You?" He backed away.

"We found him too late."

"We? Who is we?"

"Jimmy and I. We found him on the beach, barely breathing. I did all I could."

His brows drew together. His lips narrowed. He took a step toward her. "What did you give him?"

She forced herself not to shrink back. "Nothing that would harm him. You know I wouldn't."

He scrubbed at his face. Confusion clouded his eyes. Then he blinked, and all that remained was anger-laced sorrow. "My brother. I can't believe it was you who killed my brother. How long have you known and kept it a secret?"

He believed her to be a killer. His condemning words ripped through her like a wide-bladed knife. "Jacob. You know that isn't true. I only realized this man was your brother when I saw you here a day or so ago. I didn't want to tell you, because I knew you would hate me. But I cannot live a lie. You also must honor the truth. You know I did not kill your brother."

He shook his head, backing away as if he found her presence distasteful.

"Jacob." Every bit of her longing and fear poured from that word.

He held out a hand to stop her. "Don't. Just don't."

Teena's confession had shaken him to the core. Left him angry. Weak. He stumbled back to the clinic. Mack, striding by on a mission, saw him and abruptly changed direction to cross to Jacob.

"You look sick. Are you?"

"You didn't tell me Teena was the shaman who treated my brother." Mack had told him he helped bury Aaron in the churchyard.

"I assumed you knew the details. Your brother's partner was keen to be the one to tell you of his death."

"He sent a long letter. Said Aaron had been poisoned."

Mack jerked about to face Jacob. "Poisoned?"

"By a shaman."

Mack shook his head. "If he was poisoned, it wasn't by Teena. But then, you know that." His voice grew soft. "Don't you?"

Jacob didn't answer. His anger made it impossible to think.

The next day left him little chance to deal with his feelings. Teena didn't return. Not that he could blame her. Nor even that he wanted her to.

His insides felt gored, torn apart with anger and guilt.

"Doc, are you there? Got a man here."

Jacob jerked about to answer the call.

Outside, Thomas Stone held a limp body in his arms. "Found him up the mountain. Appears he's been there some time. I haven't been up there for three days."

A crowd followed Thomas, all shouting at once.

He couldn't make it out, but it was something about an accident. Or a fight. Or was it something about gold? These people would kill themselves, and each other, over the promise of gold. And according to Mack, it was worse in other towns, like Skaguay.

Mack pushed through the crowd. "What's going on?"

Jacob signaled for the injured man to be carried inside and placed on the bed next to Thad. He immediately started to examine him, while Thomas explained how he'd found the man up the trail. The raucous crowd pressed around the clinic. Several clattered into the office area.

"Stay back. No closer than the boardwalk." Mack barked out the order and the men reluctantly moved back. "So, what is all this fuss about?" He directed his question to Thomas.

Thomas shrugged, indicating he had no idea.

Mack moved to the doorway. "Who cares to tell me what's going on?"

Everyone shouted at once. Mack stopped them and, one by one, allowed a man to speak. "A fight." "Knives." Turns out this had nothing to do with Thomas Stone's man. There had been a fight on the waterfront and someone lay injured on the beach.

"I can't go down there," Jacob said. "Teena, go—" But Teena wasn't here. "Bring the injured up here. I'll tend to him."

The crowd thinned. Jacob turned his attention back to the man before him. "His ankle is swollen. Likely broken. But by the looks of it, this must have happened some days ago."

"I should have checked the trail sooner." Thomas sounded as if this was his fault.

"He'll be fortunate if he doesn't lose his foot." He probed the area.

The patient lifted his head and roared. "Leave me leg alone. Yer hurting me, man." The man was big and fought Jacob.

Thomas held the man down. "I'll stay and help."

Jacob thought of his remedies. Knew the tissue was perilously close to being gangrenous. If it got that bad, nothing but amputation would keep this man alive. He thought of Thad, and how Teena's poultice had stopped the man's infection. How one of her teas had made Burns's lungs better. Would she have something to help this man?

Margie had come in, no doubt to make sure Thad wasn't being neglected in all the commotion.

"I need Teena," Jacob said. He would not let personal reluctance put his patient at risk, even if it meant asking a shaman to help him. "Can you send for her?"

Teena hurried to the clinic, her heart thudding heavily against her chest. Jacob needed her. Surely he would see she was a healer, not a murderer. She slipped past the men hanging about the clinic, and saw the patient on the bed next to Thad's, his foot swollen and blackened.

"Can you make a poultice to help this?" Jacob didn't look at her.

She blinked back her disappointment. "I'll make

something." She hurried out to boil water and steep leaves. A crowd carried a man to the clinic. Blood dripped from his side. A slash in his shirt revealed a long knife cut. "I'll tell the doctor you need him."

She tested the concoction. It had cooled enough for her to soak clean rags in the liquid. She carried them inside to wrap about the foot. "Man outside with a knife cut."

"Stay with this one." Jacob left her and hurried out to tend the injured man. Thomas held the patient as he thrashed about.

"He is in pain," she said.

"Doc gave him something for that."

Laudanum. It began to take effect and the man calmed.

"Look what these people's greed does. God must be angry when He sees how they act." Perhaps God was punishing her for forgetting her reason for wanting to work with Jacob. To learn how to treat white man diseases, not to fill her heart with hopeless dreams.

Thomas grunted. "Not everyone is acting out of greed. For some it is desperation. Wanting to provide for their family. Besides, God loves these people. Every one of them."

"Sometimes it is hard to believe that God loves us no matter what." Right now it seemed impossible, but her thoughts hearkened back to how she'd felt after Sarah was hurt. "I disobeyed my elders when I was young, and because of it a friend was crippled. I wished I could take my choice back. I couldn't. I thought God was punishing me. Making me miserable through my friend because of my sin. Her father, the missionary, saw my agony, and one day he spoke to me. This is what he said. 'Teena, God hates sin, but he loves the sinner. Sometimes our choices have consequences, but not because God wants to hurt us. Remember the verse "While we were yet sinners, Christ died for us"? He came to save us from our sins. Not punish us for them.' I felt a lot better after that knowing God still loved me." There was scant comfort in the thought today. Yes, God loved her. But she ached for more than God's love. Would her heart ever be whole without Jacob's love?

Thomas nodded. "God is always ready to forgive. More so than we are. Isn't that right, Jacob?"

Jacob had returned. How much had he heard? She glanced at him, hoping he would understand that love could survive mistakes, misunderstandings—but his gaze was so laced with anger she could not bear it. If he'd heard Thomas, he didn't apply it to himself. Perhaps only God loved enough to forgive. "I'll wait outside." She slipped away.

"You have a way with God's word. Mack could sure use you to take over the preaching," Jacob murmured.

"Got my work cut out for me," Thomas said with determination.

Teena sank to the ground with her back to the wall of the clinic—where she could help if needed but be out of Jacob's sight. Her insides ached so bad she felt ill. She had tried to save Jacob's brother. Done all she knew. It hadn't been enough. But how could Jacob accuse her of killing him? How could he refuse to understand and forgive?

How pleasant it would be to escape the clinic and return to the spot on the trail where they sat as he read the Holy Word to her. A roar of pain grabbed her heart and squeezed so hard, the world went black for a moment. Would they ever sit together again? Would he ever read to her? Discuss what it meant?

She sucked back the pain. The place next to the marsh would remain, even though she might never again share it with Jacob. She would visit it often, letting the memory grow solid in her soul.

Weariness reached the marrow of her bones. She acknowledged it was more fatigue of the soul than of the body. Jacob only tolerated her presence because he hoped her primitive ways might help him save that man's foot. Only her concern for the injured man prevented her from leaving this place, to never return.

That, and a persistent hope he would let reason prevail. He had to know she hadn't killed his brother by either intent or ignorance.

But Jacob was a stubborn man. He didn't relinquish an idea easily.

"Teena?" She glanced toward the soft voice.

Viola, her red hair mussed, dark shadows under her eyes, held the baby, who squirmed and fussed. "Is the doctor available? I'm afraid Goldie's got that sickness your village had."

Teena's heart stalled within her chest. If Goldie was sick…

She couldn't contemplate how the illness would affect the baby. And if the baby was sick, how many others would be? She leaned her head back against the wall. If only she could protect Jacob from such a disaster.

Chapter Thirteen

Teena slowly got to her feet and led Viola to a quiet spot. "Has the baby had diarrhea?"

"Yes, some."

She asked questions about other symptoms. It didn't seem like cholera. The baby wasn't sick enough. But something was making the child fretful. "Let me see her."

Viola handed her Goldie and the baby stopped fussing, staring into Teena's face, as if wondering who was this stranger and why did she hold her.

"Hello, little one. What's making you so miserable?"

Goldie sucked in air, squeezed her eyes and let out a wail.

It gave Teena a chance to stick her finger into the baby's mouth and feel her gums. Goldie bit down on her finger then began to suck it. As soon as she did, she wailed.

Teena chuckled. "I think I know what's wrong with her. She's teething. See how swollen her gums are. I expect they are sore as boils. I can give you something for it." She waited, wondering if Viola would insist on seeing the doctor.

"Oh, if you please. I haven't slept in two days and I'm so weary I can't think straight. Just teething, you say?" She shook her head, sending the red curls hanging around her neck into a lively dance. "Why didn't I think of that?"

"Have you had a baby before Goldie?"

Viola's cheeks grabbed the pink of the evening sun. "No." Her eyes grew curious. "Have you?"

Teena chuckled. "No, but I've helped care for dozens of them." Her amusement died. Sorrow stung her eyes. So many gone now from pox and other diseases.

She reached for her bag that was never far away, and found the powder she wanted. "Mix this with a little honey and rub her gums whenever she fusses." They didn't have honey handy, so Teena moistened a bit with water and rubbed Goldie's gums. The baby sucked at the moisture. She knew the baby would soon calm.

She handed Goldie to Viola. "She'll be fine. But bring her back in the morning if you're worried."

"Thank you so much."

Viola scurried away, shielding the baby from the curious stares of those who saw her.

Thomas had stepped out of the clinic. Teena giggled at the look on his face. "You should breathe now."

Thomas drew in a long breath. "Who is that?"

She told him about Viola—the little she knew. "You like her?"

"Teena, I've never seen such a beautiful woman. She seems so vulnerable."

"I couldn't say."

"Not that I'm interested." He stared in the direction Viola had taken. "Got my work to do."

Teena took the pan from the stove where she kept the concoction warm, and headed for the clinic. At the doorway she hesitated. She had to check on the poultice. But she dreaded to face Jacob. Sucking in strengthening air, she slipped inside. "I need to soak the poultices again."

Jacob sponged the man.

"I need to soak the cloth again," she repeated when he gave no indication that he heard.

He nodded.

She tended to the poultice, then stood back. "Give it time to work."

"I appreciate this." He sat back on a chair. "I do all I can, and it is far too little."

She nodded. Waited for him to say he understood she did all she could and sometimes failed, as well.

Instead, he sighed like the weight of the mountain rested on his chest. "I can manage here if you want to leave."

"Of course." He was telling her to leave. Saying he didn't want her helping him. As if he couldn't bear to see her or talk to her. Her heart worked as efficiently as if it were made from wood.

She slipped away, disappointment nipping at her heels. Was he too prideful to admit he was wrong? Or too stubborn to believe it? Or—her heart thudded to the bottom of her insides—had he simply pushed her from his heart? Willing to let the shaman woman help because he needed her, but nothing more. After all, she was native, he was white. She sucked back air that sat foul and heavy in her lungs.

She tidied up the area about the stove, organized the eating utensils. Knew she was delaying her departure in the hope Jacob would change his mind and ask her to stay. But he did not come.

Perhaps she should check on Goldie and make sure the baby had been relieved by the powder. She hurried down the trail. Found Goldie sleeping and Viola too tired to visit. Not that Teena felt like visiting. Her heart lay torn and bleeding. Things were over between her and Jacob. He would never ask for her answer to his question about whether a white man and a Tlingit woman could marry. No point in her returning to the white man's world ever again.

She meant to stay away, but her concern over the man with the injured foot drove her back to the clinic the next morning. And a hopeless hope that Jacob might have relented in his anger toward her.

She crossed the line of men awaiting the doctor. As usual, there were those who muttered about her presence. Today, one man was especially vocal. "What's a dirty Injun doing at the clinic?"

She kept her head lowered as she darted a glance at

him. Her dress was clean, her hair tidy. She'd washed recently and often. He looked like he hadn't been within touching distance of water in a long time. Yet he called her dirty.

Several more men joined in calling her names. One threw a chunk of mud that landed at her feet, spattering her skirt. Experience told her to ignore it and continue on her way. Sometimes, however, it was hard to pretend she didn't hear, didn't care. Today she was too tired to exert common sense, and she faced the circle of mocking men.

"I am not—"

Before she could say she wasn't ignorant and unkind like many of them, the men surged forward. One laughed, the sound as cruel as a scream. They called her names, their taunting spreading like cholera, until a dozen men were pressing close, pointing fingers.

She tried to back away, but they had surrounded her. She glanced toward the clinic. Where was Jacob? He must surely have heard the uproar and the accusations. Why didn't he defend her? She faced the angry glare of those around her, silently informing them she didn't care what they thought. Any of them. A giant denial filled her heart. Except Jacob. Not that he would ever throw mud. Or call her names. But his rejection hurt a thousand times more.

Someone in the crowd shouted. "Look. Isn't that McRoy? I thought he'd made it over the mountain long ago."

The angry expressions on the faces surrounding her

suddenly shifted to curiosity, and the men surged toward the approaching McRoy, their attention diverted from tormenting Teena.

Teena waited. But still Jacob did not come out. His failure to do so could not have said how he felt more loudly if he'd stood on the top of the clinic roof and yelled to the thousands around him. She hung her head. Her father had tried to warn her she couldn't be white. But the truth was stronger than that. She couldn't even fit in with the only white man who mattered to her. Her father had said more. She recalled the gesture he'd made with his hands and said that was her task. She didn't understand then and even less now. Whatever it was, she had failed him.

Her hands were almost too heavy for her arms to hold. Her feet felt like she carried a shoe full of gold in each. Not making her happy, but weighing her so she could barely move.

She did not belong here. It took a great deal of effort to take a step forward, toward her village.

Her heavy feet made it down the walk. She had no idea where she meant to go. Only that her heart would remain forever with Jacob, even though she must move on.

At the end of the boardwalk, someone called out to her. "Ma'am, can you give me directions?"

She paused. "Where do you want to go?"

"Is there a medical clinic in town?"

"There is." Just thinking of it made her bones feel raw and naked, burning under the bright sun. She ran her gaze over the man. He practically bounced on the balls of his feet. His face glowed with excitement. "You don't look like you need a doctor."

"Don't. I *am* a doctor. I understand Dr. Calloway wants to leave. I've come to replace him." He bounced happily.

Her heart had no bounce in it. No joy. Nothing but a dreadful emptiness that would soon fill with sorrow and regret, even if she did her best to keep the door to her heart barred.

"It's over there." She pointed, her words scraping from her throat.

"Thanks." He continued on his way, so jolly it hurt to watch.

Jacob didn't intend to stay. All her hopes had been in vain. Foolish yearnings that they could work together. If she had even a flicker of hope after the way he ignored her plight at the clinic, this killed it. Her heart filled with winter darkness she knew would not end with the changing seasons. Neither spring nor summer would relieve it.

She pressed her fingers to her mouth to hold back an agonized wail. *God, if You hear a Tlingit woman, hear me now. Please. Ease my pain.*

Jacob straightened for the first time in hours. He'd had to fight both the infection and the man for the foot, but he thought he might have won.

When Thomas left last night, the patient seemed quiet. Teena's poultices seemed to be doing their job. He thought the worst was over. He half expected Thomas to return this morning, but he hadn't. Jacob had to contend with the angry, aggressive man on his own as he fought for the foot. The infection had withdrawn into an angry boil. There came a point when he knew he had to lance it. He'd called out for someone to help, but no one answered his call.

He had to act on his own and he did.

"You'll live," he informed the patient, now resting more quietly. "I think you'll keep your foot, too."

The man mumbled, his brain numbed by laudanum and fatigue.

Jacob checked his bottle of laudanum. Only because Teena had used her remedies had the bottle lasted this long. Perhaps even today the supplies would arrive on the boat.

"Hello?" Someone called from the outer room.

"I'll be right there." He washed up and made sure his patient wasn't going to throw himself from the bed. He could only spare a few minutes away until he found someone else to watch him. He went as far as the doorway, keeping half his attention on his patient. "What can I do for you?"

"It's what I can do for you. Dr. Andrew Bramley at your service." The man stepped forward and offered his hand.

Jacob shook, not quite understanding the man's meaning. Then the name registered with a jolt. "I never wrote back to you."

Andrew grinned. "I decided not to wait for a letter.

I'm anxious to get to work." He rubbed his hands together and looked around with great interest.

Jacob glanced beyond him. There had been a lot of racket outside the clinic some time ago, but he was too busy with his patient to pay it any mind, and then it had ended. "Is there no one out there? A young woman?" He expected Teena would return, if only to check on the patient.

"I spoke to a native woman on my way here. About this tall." He held out his hand at the right height for Teena.

Where had she gone? Why hadn't she come to the clinic? He couldn't explain his unease. "Do you mind watching my patient while I check on things outside?"

"My first patient. How nice."

Jacob started to correct him, then stopped. He'd deal with this later. He hurried outside. The place was practically deserted. Only the man he'd stitched up yesterday waited to have his dressing changed. "How are you doing?"

"Feeling better today, Doc."

He glanced around, but Teena was noticeably absent, and his concern grew.

"Where is everyone?" The normal crowds were missing. Thomas had disappeared. Mack hadn't come by to check on things. And where was Teena? His thoughts wailed the question.

"Can't say, though a bit ago there was a ruckus, with some men bothering Miss Teena. Then someone said something about a gold nugget and everyone disappeared. Been quiet as a grave since."

"Bothering her? How?"

"Lots of name-calling. Nasty things they said. Sounded a little rough, but I couldn't see what they were doing."

Had they hurt her? Why must people be cruel to her? "What happened to her?"

"Can't say. But if I was her, I would have hightailed it out of here but fast." He gave Jacob a hard look. "Didn't hear *you* defending that poor girl."

"I was busy with a patient."

He nodded. "I'm sure she understood." His tone said otherwise.

"I must find her."

"I should think you must, all right. Poor girl. Terrible things they said to her."

"I'll find her and explain. There's another doctor there. I'll have him keep an eye on you until I get back."

"Another doctor. You planning on going somewhere?"

"I never planned to stay." He scrubbed at his chin, realizing he hadn't shaved since early yesterday. He must look a sight. Things had seemed so simple a month ago when he arrived, but no longer did. "But now I don't know."

The last few days, he'd let his anger get in the road. Misdirected it at Teena, when really he was angry with...

He didn't even know who to be angry with. Himself, for not stopping Aaron? His parents, for letting his brother continually make foolish decisions? Aaron, for being so pigheaded? Maybe all, and yet none.

Sometimes you did all you could and it wasn't enough. At some point, a person had to leave things in God's hands and trust Him. In the most secret part of his heart, he acknowledged that even if she had been responsible for Aaron's death, it wouldn't prevent him from loving her. On one hand, the thought gave him a sense of satisfaction. Peace. Safety.

On the other hand, it filled him with bitter guilt. Was he such a poor brother? A disappointing son? Could he choose Teena over his family? But he wasn't choosing between them. He was choosing to love her.

"I have to find her." He hurried away, clomping into the clinic to inform the new doctor he needed him to help a bit longer.

Jacob hesitated at the door. "What did you say to Teena?"

"Told her I was here to take your place."

He groaned.

"Did I say something wrong?"

"Never mind. I won't be back until I find her."

He went first to her village. As he stepped from the trees, one of her old aunts barred his passage.

"Go from here," she muttered.

"I've come to see Teena."

"Go." She shooed at him.

"Teena," he bellowed at the top of his voice. A baby cried and several voices muttered protest. "Teena, I must talk to you," he called again. He called a third time, a fourth.

The old auntie narrowed her eyes. "Go away."

"I will not go until I see Teena." He yelled three more times.

From the shadows lumbered another old auntie. She spoke to the first one. They argued in their own language. He understood only Teena's name, Siteen.

"Tell me where she is."

The old ladies glared at each other. The elder nodded and waved her hand toward Jacob and gave an order. The other auntie sighed and faced Jacob, obviously not happy with the outcome. "I am to tell you she is not here. She has gone."

"Gone? Where?"

The woman waved her arm to indicate the entire world, for all Jacob knew. "She go gathering her plants."

His breath jerked from his lungs. "I'll find her." He headed back toward Treasure Creek. He'd find her if it took all day, the rest of the year, the rest of his life. He had to find her and explain how he felt. If she said she didn't welcome his love, he would accept it, but he would not rest until he told her.

His vision blurred. The thought of living without her was like planning to live without the sun, the air, the sky above. How could he do it?

Find her. Convince her.

Only, it was a mighty big place. He closed his eyes and pictured her—them—sitting next to the marsh as she told him about the plants. He'd read the Bible to her there. They had talked. And at that place, he'd felt his heart bind itself to her.

He hurried up the trail, breathless by the time he reached the spot. He ducked through the trees and broke into the open, where they had sat, where their hearts had seemed to be as one. He glanced around, hungry for a glance of her. All he saw were birds bending the reeds as they sang. "Teena." Her name was a moan from deep inside.

A rustling to one side drew his attention. Perhaps a deer startled by his presence. He peered into the shadows. Teena sat watching him, almost invisible.

He leaped to her side. "Teena?" Suddenly, all the things he wanted to say fled and he could think of nothing. He sat by her side, their shoulders brushing. "Why did you run away?"

"Why did you not tell me you were planning to leave?"

He couldn't answer before he said the things in his heart. "Teena, I didn't know the men were bothering you. I would have defended you if I did. I was busy with the patient." He explained what happened in the little room. Felt her listening. Waiting.

He swallowed hard. The words knotted in his throat, twisted with all the reasons it could not be. "I am much older than you."

"What does that matter?"

He nodded. "I am stubborn."

"I know."

She wasn't being much help.

He voiced another thought. "We could help many people if we worked together."

Slowly, she turned and met his eyes. "You want me to be your nurse? But are you staying?"

"Yes. No." He scrubbed his chin. When had speaking his mind become so difficult? "I saved that man's foot with your herbs. I helped people who had no help. I did my best. Yes, sometimes it isn't enough." Did he deserve anything from God's hands? He'd been harsh with Teena. Accused her unfairly. He'd failed again. Just as he had failed to protect Aaron. Failed in so many other ways.

"I remember what you said the other day."

She nodded. Waited.

When the sweet sense of oneness had enveloped them as he read from the Bible. "We can only do what we can do. After that we have to let go."

Her words had eased his mind about whether or not he lived up to expectations. God had none when His love was revealed in Jesus. Remembering the conversation again eased his mind. A sense of peace and purpose filled him as he lifted his head. "Teena, I don't blame you for my brother's death. It was cruel of me to do so. I wanted to blame someone, and you were handy."

"Who do you blame now?"

He smiled as peace edged into the corners of his

heart. "No one. Sometimes death is a pure waste, but there is only so much I can do. I want to learn to do more, but I no longer feel I need to fight God."

"God does more than we can, when it comes to healing."

He laughed. "Sometimes I forget that." He reached for her hand and studied her palm—so firm and yet so gentle. "Teena, I have decided to stay here and help these people. They need me. They need us."

She nodded, her gaze watchful, waiting.

"Teena, I don't know if your people would approve, but I love you and I want to marry you. Together, we can help many and we can…" he took her hands in his and held them a few inches apart "…we can bridge the gap between your people and mine." He pulled their joined hands together, fist to fist.

She gasped. "That's what Father meant."

He blinked. He'd confessed his love. Asked her to marry him—and she talked about her father?

Her gaze filled with wonder and, perching on her knees, she leaned close. "Father saw how I had come to care for you and he said it was my *task* to—but he was too weak to finish, and instead did this." She pulled her hands from his, made two fists and then drew them together in an imitation of the motion he had made. "I didn't know what he meant, but you did the same thing." She grabbed his hands and repeated the movement. "He gave me his blessing to love you and marry you." She ducked her head. "I didn't know if you cared in that way. Especially when you were so angry about Aaron." Her voice caught. "And then you didn't say anything when those people called me ugly names."

"I'm sorry." If only he could stop everyone from such behavior, but he knew he couldn't. Just as he couldn't fix everyone's injuries. It was yet another thing he would leave in God's loving hands.

He caught Teena by the shoulders and pulled her closer. "Teena, I love you. Will you marry me?"

She pressed her warm palms to his cheeks and met his eyes in a look that promised her heart. "Jacob, I love you. I will marry you and stand by your side through good and bad, and especially through the mean things people will say about us. For the rest of my life I will love you."

Her words burrowed deep into his soul, where he would cherish them always. He smiled at her, promising her his heart. "I will stand by you through good and bad, through any mean things people say and through every new challenge."

He leaned forward and sealed their vows with a kiss.

After a few minutes, she leaned back and studied his face, her eyes glowing. "I once wondered if God heard the prayers of a Tlingit as quickly as He heard a white man's prayers. Now I know He does. I asked Him to heal your anger and help you see how much you are needed here." Her gaze caressed his cheeks. "With His help, we will bridge the differences between our people."

His heart full of love and joy, he signaled his agreement with another kiss. With her he had found what he longed for all his life—a place of rest and peace.

* * * * *

Don't miss the next book in
Love Inspired Historical's Alaskan Brides series,
GOLD RUSH BABY by Dorothy Clark.

Dear Reader,

I particularly liked working on this story. I've done research on the Klondike gold rush before and used the elements in an earlier story I wrote. It even provided the impetus for a long-dreamed-of holiday to Alaska and the Yukon. I was totally blown away by the place. It is a beautiful area with a colorful history. Many of you who know the area and the history intimately will note certain discrepancies with the facts. My apologies, but they are for the sake of the story.

This story allowed me to deal with an issue that I often address—those who don't fit in, those who face prejudice. I hope I did the subject justice.

As always, I love to hear from readers. You may contact me through my website, www.lindaford.org, where you can also learn of upcoming releases. Or contact me at lindaford@airnet.com.

Blessings,

Linda Ford

QUESTIONS FOR DISCUSSION

1. Teena's people have lived in the area of the story for centuries, but now they are feeling displaced. How has that changed what Teena does or how she lives?

2. Good and bad have come with the arrival of people from the outside world. What does Teena see as good? As bad?

3. How does she cope? How do others in her clan react?

4. Are there times or events in your life that shake up your world? How do you deal with it?

5. Jacob is prejudiced. Does he realize it? At what point does his attitude change?

6. Do you feel he has a basis for the way he views Teena early in the story?

7. What is it that brings them together?

8. Are there people in your life that don't fit your idea of a proper lifestyle? For instance, the homeless, the addicted, etc. Is there a way to bridge the gap between you and them?

9. No doubt, many of those involved in this gold rush, as in any gold rush, were driven by greed. What else drove them to such extremes? Where would you place yourself in this crowd? What would drive you?

10. Jacob was trying to prove himself. To whom? And why? What did he learn about God's acceptance of him? Do you ever feel you have to bring something to God to earn His favor?

11. Teena also had questions and doubts in her spiritual walk. What were they? How did she resolve them?

12. It is unreasonable to think Teena and Jacob will not face prejudice as a couple. How do you think they will deal with it? Do you think it is possible for them to bridge the distance between their people?

13. Do you think things would change if Jacob decides to return to Seattle? How? How would you suggest they deal with it?

14. How important was the setting of this story? Did it influence the outcome?

15. Would you want to live in gold rush days? Why or why not?

INSPIRATIONAL

Inspirational romances to warm your heart & soul.

Love Inspired. HISTORICAL

TITLES AVAILABLE NEXT MONTH

Available June 14, 2011

GOLD RUSH BABY
Alaskan Brides
Dorothy Clark

MARRYING THE PREACHER'S DAUGHTER
Cheryl St.John

THE WEDDING SEASON
Deborah Hale & Louise M. Gouge

THE IRRESISTIBLE EARL
Regina Scott

REQUEST YOUR FREE BOOKS!

2 FREE INSPIRATIONAL NOVELS
PLUS 2
FREE
MYSTERY GIFTS

Love Inspired

HISTORICAL
INSPIRATIONAL HISTORICAL ROMANCE

YES! Please send me 2 FREE Love Inspired® Historical novels and my 2 FREE mystery gifts (gifts are worth about $10). After receiving them, if I don't wish to receive any more books, I can return the shipping statement marked "cancel". If I don't cancel, I will receive 4 brand-new novels every month and be billed just $4.24 per book in the U.S. or $4.74 per book in Canada. That's a saving of at least 23% off the cover price. It's quite a bargain! Shipping and handling is just 50¢ per book in the U.S. and 75¢ per book in Canada.* I understand that accepting the 2 free books and gifts places me under no obligation to buy anything. I can always return a shipment and cancel at any time. Even if I never buy another book, the two free books and gifts are mine to keep forever.

102/302 IDN FDCH

Name	(PLEASE PRINT)	

Address		Apt. #

City	State/Prov.	Zip/Postal Code

Signature (if under 18, a parent or guardian must sign)

Mail to the **Reader Service:**
IN U.S.A.: P.O. Box 1867, Buffalo, NY 14240-1867
IN CANADA: P.O. Box 609, Fort Erie, Ontario L2A 5X3

Not valid for current subscribers to Love Inspired Historical books.

Want to try two free books from another series?
Call 1-800-873-8635 or visit www.ReaderService.com.

* Terms and prices subject to change without notice. Prices do not include applicable taxes. Sales tax applicable in N.Y. Canadian residents will be charged applicable taxes. Offer not valid in Quebec. This offer is limited to one order per household. All orders subject to credit approval. Credit or debit balances in a customer's account(s) may be offset by any other outstanding balance owed by or to the customer. Please allow 4 to 6 weeks for delivery. Offer available while quantities last.

Your Privacy—The Reader Service is committed to protecting your privacy. Our Privacy Policy is available online at www.ReaderService.com or upon request from the Reader Service.

We make a portion of our mailing list available to reputable third parties that offer products we believe may interest you. If you would prefer that we not exchange your name with third parties, or if you wish to clarify or modify your communication preferences, please visit us at www.ReaderService.com/consumerschoice or write to us at Reader Service Preference Service, P.O. Box 9062, Buffalo, NY 14269. Include your complete name and address.

LIH11

With time running out to stop the Lions of Texas
from orchestrating their evil plan, Texas Ranger
Levi McDonall must work with his childhood friend
to solve his captain's murder and thwart the group's
disastrous plot. Read on for a preview of OUT OF TIME
by Shirlee McCoy, the exciting conclusion to the
TEXAS RANGER JUSTICE *series.*

Silence told its own story, and Susannah Jorgenson listened as she hurried across the bridge that led to the Alamo Chapel. Darkness had fallen hours ago and the air held a hint of rain. The shadows seemed deeper than usual, the darkness just a little blacker. Or maybe it was simply her imagination that made the Alamo complex seem so forbidding.

She shivered. Not from the cold. Not from the chilly breeze. From the darkness, the silence, the endless echo of her fear as she made her final rounds. She jogged to the chapel and flashed the beam of her light along the corners of the building.

Nothing.

No movement, no sounds, no reason to think she wasn't alone, but she couldn't shake the feeling that she was being watched. That somewhere beyond the beam of her light, danger waited. She did a full sweep of the chapel and of the office area beyond. Nothing, of course.

She opened the chapel door, stepping straight into a broad, muscular chest. Someone grabbed her upper arms, holding her in place.

She shoved forward into her attacker, pushing her weight into a solid wall of strength as she tried to unbalance him.

"Calm down. I was just trying to keep you from falling." The man released his hold.

"Sorry about that. I wasn't expecting anyone to be standing near the door. We're closed for the day, but we'll be open again at seven tomorrow morning." She cleared her throat.

"No need to apologize. I'm Ranger Levi McDonall. My captain said he was going to call and let you know I was on the way."

"Levi McDonall?" Her childhood idol? Her best guy friend? Her first teenage crush?

No way could they be the same.

"Come on in." She hurried into the chapel, trying to pull herself together. This was the Texas Ranger she'd be working with for the next eight days?

She flipped on a light, turned to face McDonall.

Levi McDonall.

Her Levi McDonall.

*Can Levi and Susannah put the past behind them
to save San Antonio's future? Find out in OUT OF TIME
by Shirlee McCoy from Love Inspired Suspense,
available in June wherever books are sold.*

HISTORICAL

INSPIRATIONAL HISTORICAL ROMANCE

Wedding bells will ring in these two romantic
Regency stories from two favorite
Love Inspired Historical authors.
'Tis the season for falling in love!

The Wedding Season

by DEBORAH HALE *and* LOUISE M. GOUGE

Available June wherever books are sold.